Emily Harvale lives in Ea
although she would prefe1
Alps...or Canada...or anywhere that has several
months of snow. Emily loves snow almost as much
as she loves Christmas.

Having worked in the City (London) for several
years, Emily returned to her home town of Hastings
where she spends her days writing. And wondering
if it will snow.

You can contact her via her website, Twitter,
Facebook or Instagram.

There is also a Facebook group where fans can chat
with Emily about her books, her writing day and life
in general. Details are on the 'For You' page of
Emily's website.

Author contacts:
www.emilyharvale.com
www.twitter.com/emilyharvale
www.facebook.com/emilyharvalewriter
www.instagram.com/emilyharvale

***

Scan the code above to see all Emily's books on Amazon

Also by this author

Highland Fling
Lizzie Marshall's Wedding
The Golf Widows' Club
Sailing Solo
Carole Singer's Christmas
Christmas Wishes
A Slippery Slope
The Perfect Christmas Plan
Be Mine
It Takes Two
Bells and Bows on Mistletoe Row

The Goldebury Bay series:
Ninety Days of Summer – book 1
Ninety Steps to Summerhill – book 2
Ninety Days to Christmas – book 3

The Hideaway Down series:
A Christmas Hideaway – book 1
Catch A Falling Star – book 2
Walking on Sunshine – book 3
Dancing in the Rain – book 4

Hall's Cross series
Deck the Halls – book 1
The Starlight Ball – book 2

Michaelmas Bay series
Christmas Secrets in Snowflake Cove – book 1
Blame it on the Moonlight – book 2

Lily Pond Lane series
The Cottage on Lily Pond Lane –
Part One – New beginnings and Summer secrets
Part Two – Autumn leaves and Trick or treat
Christmas on Lily Pond Lane
Return to Lily Pond Lane
A Wedding on Lily Pond Lane
Secret Wishes and Summer Kisses on Lily Pond Lane

Wyntersleap series
Christmas at Wynter House – book 1

Merriment Bay series
Coming Home to Merriment Bay – book 1

New Beginnings
at
Wynter House

Emily Harvale

ISBN 978-1-909917-54-5

Published by Crescent Gate Publishing

Print edition published worldwide 2020
E-edition published worldwide 2020

Editor Christina Harkness

Cover design by JR and Emily Harvale

To Eileen.
Some friendships last a lifetime and true friends are there to pick up the pieces when we fall and to stand us up again so that we can face the world.

Chapter One

Neva smiled into her phone even though her best friend, Jo couldn't see her face.

'This was my best Christmas ever,' she said. 'Rafe is definitely 'The One' as far as I'm concerned. I hope he's not having second thoughts. What will I do if he dumps me?'

'You're a nutter.' Jo tutted loudly and added a sigh, no doubt to emphasise her point. 'Why would he dump you? From what you've told me the guy's as crazy about you as you are about him. And he gave you a family heirloom as a Christmas present. You don't give someone a locket that belonged to your great, great, great-grandmother, if you think you might not stay with them for the long haul.'

'True. But that was really a little joke. Because when he found me lying on the ground, trying to peer into the old barn the other night, I said I was looking for my locket, and he said he knew I didn't have one. He gave me this beautiful heirloom so that I could at least have a locket I could pretend to lose.

Although he did ask me to be careful not to actually lose it if possible.'

Neva tucked the oval locket beneath her jumper, smiling at the memory of how she had, for one brief moment, suspected Rafe of being a drug dealer ... or worse.

'A gold and diamond locket, that's probably worth more than the price of a house, judging by the photo you sent me, is *not* a little joke, Neva. I think the guy's pretty serious about you.'

'But that's the thing. I can't believe my luck. I'm half expecting to wake up and find this was all some wonderful dream. I keep pinching myself.'

'All that'll do is give you bruises. Stop worrying about things that will probably never happen and get on with enjoying yourself with your gorgeous new man. I can't wait to meet him. And his yummy-sounding brother. He's still single, yes?'

'Since I spoke to you yesterday? Yes. Adam's still single. But something weird happened today and that's why I had to call you.'

'Oh? Here's me thinking it was because you're my best friend and you wanted to check how I am. And that I haven't murdered my fiancé and his awful mother yet.' Jo sighed again.

'I do. And I know you haven't because if

you had you would've called to tell me. How are things though?'

'Let's just say this was probably my second worst Christmas ever. Nothing could be as bad as the Christmases with my mum and dad, but this one came pretty close. I meant what I said, Neva. Unless something miraculous happens between now and the New Year, Rob and I are history.'

'And I meant what I said. There's a second bedroom in my new flat in Merriment Bay and having you join me in my new business would be a dream come true. I'm not saying I want your relationship to end, but I am saying that I honestly think it may be for the best. If you really loved Rob, you wouldn't let his mum come between you. Olivia Wynter clearly detests me, and if looks could kill, I'd have been deader than yesterday's Christmas goose, and buried several times over during Christmas dinner. But I'm not going to let her scare me off. You know the saying. 'Love Rafe, love his bitchy old gran.' That's going to be my morning mantra.'

'Or you could get Sasha to spend a day with her. That'd probably give her a heart attack. You're right about me and Rob. I do love him. I just don't love him enough. I shouldn't have said yes when he proposed, and I definitely shouldn't have agreed to move in with him. That was a mistake. But on the bright side, if I hadn't, we wouldn't have sold our flat and your mum and dad wouldn't have given you your fab present of a new flat and a new salon in Merriment Bay. It was clearly meant to be. Plus it's made me realise that marriage is probably not for me.'

'Or it's because you haven't met 'The One' yet.'

'Maybe. Anyway, what were you saying? Something weird happened? Weird how? Is this about sex? Don't tell me Rafe's into all that kinky stuff. It's always the quiet ones.'

'No. It's not about sex. The sex is out of this world. In a good way. This is something else. We went to the Boxing Day dip in Merriment Bay. Rafe, me, Rowan, Nigel and Sasha and ... well, all of us. But not Ethel and Queenie. Or Mum and Dad.'

'I don't really need to know who went. It could take all day. What's the Boxing Day dip?'

Neva laughed. 'It's a tradition. Everyone goes for a swim in the sea in Merriment Bay on Boxing Day.'

'OK. That *is* weird.'

Neva tutted. 'That's not the weird bit. Well, maybe it's a little weird but it was actually fun. And once I got the feeling back in my feet and hands and stopped my teeth from chattering, I enjoyed it.'

'*You're* weird.'

'Says the woman hiding in the garden shed

to avoid talking to her fiancé's mum. Anyway, there's this guy called Amias Wells. He's a friend of Rafe and Adam and he owns a water sports centre on the beach and a fantastic house overlooking the bay. Oooooh. He's gorgeous. And single, I believe. Although he did take some stunning woman called Diana off to see the local museum.'

'Is that a euphemism for having sex?'

'No. He really did take her to see the WWII Museum.'

'Gosh. He sounds like fun. I mean, who wouldn't want to go to some old museum?'

'It's interesting. And what's this sudden obsession with sex?'

'It's not sudden. I've always been obsessed with sex. That's half the problem. I haven't had any since Rob's delightful family arrived. He says the walls aren't that thick and he doesn't want his mum to hear me scream. I pointed out, as tactfully as I could, that it's been a while since he's made me scream, but it didn't seem to help. To be honest, there's more chance of Charmaine doing that than Rob. Only not in a good way, you understand. This relationship is doomed. Doomed, I tell you.'

Jo cackled like a witch. She always made jokes when something bad was happening in her life. It was her way of dealing with her problems.

'I'm sorry, Jo.'

'Don't be. I'm fine. So, we've established that everyone in Merriment Bay is mad and that this guy, Amias, likes museums. Are you saying something else weird happened?'

'Yes. Amias told his friends, which included us, that we were all welcome to use his place to shower and get changed. Not everyone did, but while we were there, happily chatting and drinking brandy – just to warm us up – this really pretty, tall teenager with long, ginger hair walks past, and there's suddenly this look of shock on Adam's face and he breaks off mid-sentence and dashes after her.'

'Damn. Does that mean he's now fallen madly in love with someone too?'

'No. It wasn't that sort of look. And I can't see Adam falling for a teenager. But he looked almost angry when he came back. He took Rafe to one side and whispered something. Then with just a quick look at me, Rafe goes off with Adam to talk to this girl and when they come back, they both look really confused and cross and, well … completely distracted. We were supposed to go to The Hope and Anchor after the dip, for drinks and lunch but instead Rafe asked me if I'd mind if he left us with Gavin and Julia and the others because something had come up and he and Adam needed to have an urgent word with Olivia. I haven't seen either of them since. We've been back for nearly an hour and when I asked Carruthers where Rafe was, he did that thing with his eyebrows and said that Mr Rafe and Mr Adam were with their grandmother and had given strict instructions not to be disturbed.'

'OK. That is a bit odd. I can't wait to meet Carruthers. He sounds like such a hoot.'

'He is. But he doesn't know it. Anyway. I said something facetious like, what? Not even if there's a fire or something. He said, "No, Miss Grey. I do beg your pardon. Neva. I can handle any eventuality such as that." And I really think he could. Although he still can't seem to remember to call me Neva and not Miss Grey. But anyway, it's a bit annoying.'

'Er. This girl was a teenager, you said?'

'Yeah. She looked about eighteen or so.'

'Um. You don't think she could've been either Adam or Rafe's love child, do you?'

Neva gasped.

'What? No. Er. I don't know. Oh my God! Do you think that could be it? She didn't look anything like either of them though. They're both dark haired with blue eyes. She had ginger hair and green eyes. Really stunning green eyes. I noticed them when she hurried past me, leaving Rafe and Adam staring after her as if they'd seen a ghost or something. The only thing she had in common with either of them, was the fact they're all tall. But now that I think about it, there was something about the shape of her face. She had their confidence too. You could see that in the way she walked.'

'Well, that's it then. She's tall and confident and has a similar shaped face. Yep. She's the kid of one of them.' Jo laughed again.

'Oh funny. You were the one who suggested it, not me. But it must be something like that, mustn't it? Or something big. I mean really big. Because I'm not kidding, when I said both Rafe and Adam looked shocked, confused and cross, they really did. Add to that the fact they've been locked away with Olivia all afternoon and it's clear there's definitely something huge going on.'

'OK. But when Rafe eventually resurfaces, you can just ask him, can't you? He did tell you about his gin distillery and took you to the old barn so that you could see it for yourself. And he said he didn't want there to be any secrets between you two, didn't he? So whatever it is, he'll tell you about it. And right after he does, you'll phone and tell me. Even if it's some deep, dark family secret that's suddenly come to light. In fact, especially if it's some deep, dark family secret. I need something to brighten up this bloody miserable Boxing Day, and there's nothing quite like a massive scandal in someone else's family to do that.'

Chapter Two

Adam leant back in his chair in Olivia's private sitting room and stared from her to his elder brother, Rafe, turning the glass of brandy round and round in his hand to try to keep his temper in check.

Like Rafe, he rarely lost his temper, but when he did, he did it in style. At the moment, total astonishment was the only emotion he was experiencing, and had been since Olivia had finally told them the truth, after refusing for almost an hour, to confirm or deny anything.

She had told them several stories regarding their father, Phillip, including how he had been an unhappy child, teenager and adult. How, where and when he had met their mother. Why everyone apart from Phillip had seen he was making a mistake by marrying her. How hopeless he had always been with financial matters. That he drank far too much and even dabbled with 'illegal substances' and that his untimely death had come as no great surprise to her. She talked about everything except the question they had raised. Until Rafe made it clear that he was growing increasingly tired of her prevarication and demanded she give them an answer.

But when she had, he and Rafe just stared at her and at one another in silence.

Only once he was sure he could speak without shouting at Olivia, did he attempt to do so, but first he emptied his glass and reached for the decanter to refill it.

'Well, this Christmas just keeps on giving. First Rafe meets the love of his life, and now we discover we have a sister that neither of us knew existed until today. And a niece. I'm thrilled by the added knowledge that our sister was born the same year as me. Dad really was a busy boy, wasn't he?'

Rafe threw him a look, somewhere between sympathy and fury. Olivia glowered at him.

'Denigrating your father and being sarcastic doesn't help anyone, Adam. Your father was a romantic in his way, but he was a weak man, I'll admit.'

'So it's fine for you to criticise him, but not for me?'

'He was my son.'

'And he was my father. And also, it seems, several other people's, too.'

'Adam!' Olivia's glare intensified. 'That's

unjust. As far as I am aware, Catherine Devon is his only other offspring.'

Rafe spoke at last and his tone clearly reflected his mood.

'As far as you are aware?'

He was obviously far from pleased by Olivia's revelation, but like Adam, he seemed to be keeping control of his emotions.

Olivia gave a small cough.

'I am certain Catherine Devon is the only one. If there had been others, Phillip would have told me, I assure you.'

Adam let out a derisive laugh.

'What a comfort.'

He couldn't help himself. He was only five when his mother ran off with a Count, never to contact the family again, and just six when his father died, from a combination of alcohol and drugs. Adam hardly knew him, but this felt like a betrayal of equal standing to the man having, effectively, taken his own life. Although his death was deemed accidental. And it was something the Wynters never discussed.

'Why didn't you tell us?' Rafe asked, his voice still relatively calm but cold.

Olivia stuck out her chin and smoothed down her skirt with the hand still bandaged from her accident with her wine glass just a few days ago.

'Because I dealt with it, so there was no need for you to know.'

'No need for us to know?' Rafe got to his feet as he boomed out the words. 'We have a sister and a niece and you feel there was *no need* for us to know this fact? You are unbelievable, Grandmother.'

He was clearly furious now. He only called Olivia 'Grandmother' when he was really angry and Adam couldn't remember the last time Rafe had done that.

Even yesterday, when Olivia had behaved appallingly towards Neva, making it abundantly obvious that, in her opinion, Rafe shouldn't be dating 'a hairdresser', Rafe had merely narrowed his eyes, smiled and said, 'But Neva is an excellent hairdresser, Olivia.'

And later, when Adam had heard Olivia tell Rafe that giving such a valuable family trinket as a gold and diamond locket to 'the girl' was tantamount to lunacy, Rafe had smiled sardonically and kept his temper in check.

'I intend to give Neva a great deal more of our family heirlooms,' Rafe had said. 'I suggest you come to terms with that fact, Olivia, and save yourself, and us, a lot of unnecessary unpleasantness.'

Now, Rafe was glaring at Olivia as if he could cheerfully wring her neck.

Olivia glared at him.

'You may think it is acceptable to drag the family name through the mud, Rafe, but I do not. Our monetary matters being bandied about due to my son's lack of financial acumen was bad enough. If you think I was going to add to the mockery and derision by making it public knowledge that he lacked integrity, you are deluded. Your mother running off with that dreadful Count, followed by your father deciding ... your father's untimely death did enough damage to our standing. Then, of course, there was your marriage, just as we were finally recovering our reputation. And now this new girl. It's as if you want this family to be a laughing stock.'

'Grandmother! That's enough. I have tolerated your arrogance and bitterness until now, but this new revelation, in addition to your unkindness to Neva, is making it increasingly difficult for me to remember that I care for you. Whether you like it or not, Wynter House now belongs to me, and I love Neva. She'll be spending a great deal of time here, and hopefully one day, this will be her home. If living under the same roof as us makes you unhappy, may I suggest that once the cottages in the village dry out, you move to one of the rental cottages to live?'

'Rafe! No! You cannot be serious.'

Olivia turned deathly pale and clutched a hand to her chest, her eyes bulging in horror and her mouth open in shock.

'Rafe?' Adam got up and stood between his brother and Olivia. He placed a hand on Rafe's shoulder. 'You have every right to be cross. God knows, I'm furious too. But we both know it's Olivia's way. I agree that this last piece of news is a body blow and I'm as angry as you that we've been kept in the dark over this. But it wasn't just Olivia who kept this from us. It was also Mother and Father. Olivia said they both decided, along with her, that it should remain a secret. Sending her to live in the village is a bit harsh, isn't it?' He forced a grin. 'I thought you liked the villagers.'

Rafe met Adam's eyes and after a moment or two, he grinned back, albeit only briefly.

'You're right. The villagers have had to put up with being flooded out of their homes, they shouldn't have to put up with Grandmother living in such close proximity when it's eventually safe for them to return.' He glanced at Olivia. 'You can stay. But there are going to have to be ... Grandmother? ... Olivia?'

He darted a look at Adam and they both rushed to Olivia's chair. Her eyes were closed, her arms had fallen to her side, her head was tilted forwards, and she was slumped in the chair.

'Olivia?' Adam echoed Rafe's concern.

Rafe pulled out his phone as he searched for a pulse, requesting an ambulance when the emergency services answered his call, and mouthing to Adam, to text Carruthers.

Chapter Three

Neva had only just ended her call with Jo and was leaving the library where she'd been sitting on the window seat looking out across the grounds and the melting snow, when Julia Thorn, the housekeeper-cum-Rafe and Olivia's assistant, and Archibald Carruthers, the butler dashed from separate rooms and ran across the grandiose hall to the sweep of stairs.

'What's wrong?'

It was obvious from the expression on Julia's face, at least, that something bad had happened. Carruthers' expression was as shielded as always and not even his eyebrows did their usual dance when he turned briefly to look at Neva.

'Mrs Wynter is unwell. Mr Rafe has called for an ambulance.'

'An ambulance?'

Neva's shriek echoed in her ears and she raced up the stairs, following behind Julia and Carruthers. She hadn't been to Olivia's suite of rooms so had no idea where they were going but when they arrived at the doorway of a seemingly spacious, lavender and soft grey, sitting room, all three of them stopped at the wide-open door and Carruthers tapped gently before Neva heard Rafe's voice.

'Come in, Archie. I can't hear the ambulance yet but at least Olivia is breathing. Julia, will you please pack a few things in an overnight bag in case she is admitted.'

'Of course,' Julia replied, and made her way through the sitting room to another room next door.

'Neva?'

Rafe seemed surprised to see her as she stepped inside the room. He was crouched beside a chair, holding one of Olivia's hands in his, with Adam standing beside them. Slumped in the chair in front of a roaring fire, Olivia looked more like a rag doll than the fearsome battleaxe she had been just yesterday.

'Is there anything I can do to help? She's going to be OK, isn't she?'

Rafe smiled wanly. 'I hope so. She's strong. We're hoping she's merely fainted and that it's nothing more serious. But she's had a nasty shock. My fault, entirely.'

'It wasn't your fault,' Adam snapped. 'But I know you'll still blame yourself, no matter what I say. At least let me bear half of the responsibility. I was the one who made a joke about the villagers.'

'The villagers?' Neva looked from Rafe to Adam.

What on earth was going on?

Rafe shook his head. 'It's not important right now. Please don't take this the wrong way, Neva, but I think it might be better if you weren't here when Olivia comes round. Perhaps you'd ask Penny or Taryn to go ahead with afternoon tea, without us.'

'Afternoon tea?'

Was he for real? Olivia not wanting her in the room, she could understand, but the woman looked as if she was knocking on death's door and waiting for an answer. For Rafe to be thinking about something as irrelevant as afternoon tea was beyond weird. But then, he did take his position as 'Lord of the Manor' extremely seriously. That much had become apparent to Neva since she'd met him just a few short days ago. It was actually one of the many reasons she had fallen in love with him.

Adam smiled at her.

'It's best if we behave as though everything is fine, Neva. We don't want everybody worrying.'

'Er. I hate to point this out but I think that ship has sailed. Don't you think an ambulance turning up is going to make people worried?'

Rafe frowned and Adam nodded.

Carruthers raised one eyebrow and

lowered the other, in his usual way.

'I'll deal with that, if I may, sir.' Carruthers glanced at Rafe. 'I'll say Mrs Wynter is feeling a trifle unwell and the ambulance is simply a precaution. Mrs Pyke's tea will soon distract our guests, and perhaps I might ask Miss Small to give us a cheery tune or two, for Boxing Day, if that is acceptable?'

'Excellent, Archie.' Rafe stood upright.

Carruthers didn't wait for any further instructions as he marched towards the hall.

'I'll bring the paramedics up. I believe I can hear the siren.'

'Would you like me to accompany you, Rafe?' Julia asked, a small holdall in one hand.

'Yes please. In case Olivia needs you. Adam? Are you coming with me or do you want to take your own car?'

'I'll follow in mine. Probably best in case one of us needs to return to get anything.'

'Good thinking.' Rafe nodded at him.

'I'll get out of the way then,' Neva said, turning to leave. 'I'll see if Penny or Taryn need any help.'

'Neva?' Rafe strode across the room in just a few steps and was in front of her before she knew it.

'Yes?' She looked up at him and was relieved to see him smile, albeit somewhat sadly.

'I'm sorry.'

'What for?'

He shrugged. 'For this.' He waved an arm aimlessly in the air. 'For asking you to leave the room. For abandoning you so abruptly today.'

She smiled back. 'It's not your fault Olivia doesn't like me, Rafe. And you didn't exactly abandon me. I would like to know what's happened but I know you'll tell me, if and when you can. I truly hope Olivia's OK. I'll get out of here before she comes round.'

She stood on her tiptoe and kissed him on his cheek. He looked genuinely surprised, but equally pleased. As if he still wasn't quite accustomed to the fact that they were in love. She turned to go but he grabbed her hand and pulled her into his arms.

'I love you, Neva.' He gave her the briefest kiss on her lips and quickly released her, glancing towards Olivia's chair.

'I love you too. Please let me know how Olivia is, once you're at the hospital.' She turned to walk away.

'I'll call you as soon as I can,' he said.

Neva made her way downstairs, moving aside to let Carruthers and the paramedics pass her on the staircase.

Sasha came dashing out from drawing room, looking very excited and Tempest charged after her, the dog's huge paws sliding on the polished, oak floor and no doubt leaving several more scratch marks.

'Has someone died?' Sasha jumped up and down.

'Sasha!' Neva scowled at her. 'Death isn't something you should be getting excited about. Keep your voice down, please. Olivia has been taken ill and Rafe and Adam are upset. The last thing they want to see is an eight-year-old bouncing up and down with joy at the prospect of having another ghost in this house.'

Sasha pulled a face and stuck out her bottom lip but she stood still, so that was something.

'Is she very ill?'

Neva tutted. 'I mean it, Sasha. It's not a good thing. We want Olivia to be OK.'

'But earlier you said you'd like to strangle the bloody woman. And I told you to put money in a swear jar, like the one we have for Mummy.'

'Shush! I'd like to damn well strangle you right now.'

Neva grabbed Sasha's hand and half marched, half dragged her towards the kitchen, Tempest barking and charging to and fro as if unsure whether to protect Sasha or play some sort of game.

'You can't,' Sasha said, grinning up at Neva. 'Mummy and Daddy would be cross.'

'I wouldn't bet on that, sweetie. After that business with Carruthers and the hand, and then yesterday, during Christmas dinner, going into detail about exactly how to kill a zombie and what comes out of one when they die, not to mention putting those, imitation eyeball, sweets into everyone's cocktails last night. I think your mum and dad would thank me.'

Sasha grinned triumphantly; no doubt still greatly amused by the memory of her little tricks. Especially Carruthers and the hand, and everyone's reaction to the eyeball sweets. Ronnie's in particular. On seeing an extremely lifelike eyeball 'staring' at him from his second G&T, he shrieked and threw the contents of his glass in the air. The gin and tonic saturated Cecil, who was none too pleased, and the eyeball hit Judith on her neck then dropped down the front of her dress. Adam had offered to retrieve it, which had made Judith blush profusely and dash from the room. The little joke had cost Sasha a very early night, with only a sandwich for dinner, but she seemed to think it was worth it, and regaled Ethel and Queenie with the story at breakfast, in case they had missed it.

'Are you in a bad mood?' Sasha asked, skipping along the hall, beside Neva. 'Have you and Rafe had a row? Is it about sex? Mummy and Daddy had a row about sex on Christmas morning. Daddy said he was too tired and Mummy said Daddy was giving this house more time and love than her.'

'Sasha!' Neva stopped in her tracks and

stared at her niece. 'Let me give you a piece of advice, sweetie. It's not always wise to repeat everything you hear. Or think you hear, OK?'

'OK'. Sasha shrugged, and with her hand still in Neva's, continued as before towards the kitchen. 'They had sex last night. They thought I was asleep but I wasn't.'

Neva tried not to grin. 'What did I just say to you?'

'That it's not always wise to repeat everything I hear.'

'And what did you just do?'

'I decided not to take any notice. That's what Daddy sometimes does when Mummy gives him advice. Why are you taking me to the kitchen?'

'I'm hoping Penny has a pot big enough to stick you in.'

'OK.'

Neva gave a burst of laughter. 'OK? You're one crazy kid, do you know that, Sasha?'

Sasha beamed at her. 'Yes. People are always saying that. And Mrs Drummond said I'm incorrigible.'

'Yes. I remember you telling me. It's not really a good thing, sweetie.'

Sasha shrugged again, clearly not in the least bit bothered by that fact.

'I hope there's some Christmas cake left from yesterday. That was so yummy, wasn't it? I wish I could live here forever. I don't want to go home to our house, especially as Granny and Gramps are moving away. It's not going to be anywhere near as much fun with just me and Tempest and Mummy and Daddy. Do you think, if I'm really good, Rafe might let me stay?'

Neva smiled at her. 'I think you've got about as much chance of that happening as I have of Olivia giving me her blessing to marry Rafe.'

Sasha let go of Neva's hand and ran ahead. 'I'm going to ask him, anyway. And Olivia may be dead soon.'

'Sasha!'

What was the point? As Mrs Drummond, Sasha's headmistress had said, the child was incorrigible.

Chapter Four

Word of the ambulance, and of Olivia's condition, soon reached every corner of Wynter House, and Sasha wasn't the only one who seemed inappropriately excited by this news. Especially when Neva announced during dinner that Rafe had called to say Olivia would be spending the next two days in hospital. Neva couldn't provide anyone with much more information because Rafe's call had been brief and to the point. It was as if he hadn't wanted to talk about it. But that was probably understandable.

Penny Pyke, the cook at Wynter House, and Taryn Small, the general help, served a delicious turkey curry for dinner.

Cecil and Ronnie breathed a united sigh of relief, due partly, they said, to the fact that the curry didn't contain raisins.

'Raisins have no place in a curry,' Cecil said. 'Two days, you say? Well, that's something, I suppose. We should be grateful Olivia will pull through. For Rafe and Adam's sakes, if not for ours. And it does mean that for a short while at least, we can walk our darling Persephone on her lead without fear of being subjected to one of Olivia's icy stares. And even icier comments.'

Ethel shook her head. 'How awful. Particularly at this time of year.'

Queenie gave her a sideways glance. 'Don't tell me you're mellowing towards Olivia in your old age.'

Ethel raised both brows and gave a broad, and as usual, toothless grin. 'Olivia? I wasn't thinking of her. I was feeling sorry for the doctors and nurses. They've had enough to do over the holidays, I expect, without the added trauma of dealing with Olivia Wynter.'

Neva's mum, Dawn, shook her head. 'I hope Olivia makes a full and speedy recovery. Did Rafe say exactly what happened, sweetheart?'

'No. They were having a ... discussion and one minute, Olivia was fine, the next, she was deathly pale and unresponsive.'

'The woman's always pale and unresponsive,' Rowan mumbled.

Neva frowned at her sister. 'Don't be mean about my boyfriend's grandmother.'

Ronnie made a face and looked very pleased with himself. 'What you mean, darling, is they were having a row, not a discussion. Cecil and I distinctly heard raised voices when we were walking Persephone this afternoon and happened to be passing Olivia's rooms.'

Ethel cast them an accusatory glance. 'Aren't Olivia's rooms off limits to us peasants? Happened to be passing? Or went out of your way to eavesdrop?'

Ronnie bristled. 'We took a wrong turn. This house is so large and although we've been here a few days, we're still uncertain of our bearings.'

Ethel cackled. 'That's a likely story, boys. You're lucky Olivia didn't see you or she would've given you your bearings. Right out the front door, never to set foot in Wynter House again.'

'Were they arguing?' Dawn queried, although she looked a little surprised that she'd asked that question. 'Not that it's any of my business, of course.'

Penny gave a small sigh, but it was loud enough for Neva and Dawn to hear.

'Mrs Wynter's hearing isn't quite what it was. Sometimes she raises her voice without realising.'

'Fiddle faddle.' Ethel snapped at her daughter. 'You don't have to defend the woman, Penny. She's perfectly capable of taking care of herself. And she's raised her voice to both you and me many a time, so let's not call a wolf a puppy.'

'This curry is delicious, love.' Penny's

husband, Roger beamed at her, clearly trying to change the subject.

'It's actually Wendy's recipe,' Penny said. 'It's the one she and Sean serve in Wyntersleap Inn on Friday nights.'

Gavin, the estate manager at Wynter House shook his head and gave a sad little smile as he looked at Wendy and Sean.

'I wonder how long it'll be before you're up and running again. Rafe said the insurers will organise dehumidifiers once the water levels have dropped completely and there's no further risk of flooding, but it'll still take some time for the pub and cottages to dry out. Plus they'll have to be checked for health and safety, and probably redecorated. It could be weeks.'

Sean nodded and sighed.

'Or even months.'

'Months?' Roger looked surprised. 'It's a good thing we've got some savings then, and that Penny works here. Keeping the shop shut for months isn't quite what I'd expected. I thought it'd be sorted out in a week or two and we could all move back to the village. Could it really take that long?'

Gavin nodded and glanced at George, the former estate manager and gardener at Wynter House.

'George and I went down with Rafe, Adam and Sean to take a look this morning and although the river's receded, the snow's now beginning to melt, and that could mean more problems. The ground is completely sodden so there's nowhere for the melt water to go apart from through and around the village.'

'Gavin's right,' George said. 'In all my years, I've never seen anything like this. I don't think any of us will be going home for a while.'

Cecil and Ronnie exchanged anxious glances. Ethel chuckled and pointed at them.

'You two had better not upset Olivia when she gets back, or you'll have nowhere else to go. I might offer to look after your Persephone. She's quite cute. For a cat.'

'Olivia might die,' Sasha said, standing up and trying to help herself to another portion of curry.

'Sasha!' Nigel, Rowan and Neva all glared at her.

'I do hope not,' Dennis said. 'Sweetheart? Did Rafe say anything other than that Olivia would be in hospital for a couple of days?'

Neva smiled wanly at her dad. 'He said that she'd had another ECG on arrival and the results confirmed she'd had a mild heart attack as the paramedics had said. The doctor had taken a blood sample, to check for cardiac markers, or something, and he'd told Rafe that Olivia would need to remain in the hospital for a few days while they ran more blood tests to check her troponin levels, along with other tests. I have no idea what that meant, but Rafe seemed to. Then he said he had to go and he'd be home when he could but that we should all carry on without him and Adam for the time being. And that if we needed anything, we could ask Carruthers. Or Judith when she gets back from the hospital. Which should be soon because Rafe said he would be putting her in a taxi just after we spoke. And that was more than half an hour ago.'

'A mild heart attack isn't exactly good news,' Penny said. 'But it could have been so much worse. I don't expect we'll see Rafe and Adam for another few hours. They'll be starving when they get back. I'm sure neither of them will think to eat. I've saved enough curry for them. And for Judith and Carruthers, of course. I know Carruthers didn't go to the hospital but I haven't laid eyes on him since the ambulance left. I suppose he's busy doing something or other, knowing him.'

Ethel grinned. 'Adam will be pleased. Turkey curry is his favourite.'

'I can see why.' Nigel took Sasha's plate and, despite her comment about Olivia, gave her a second helping, giving himself and Rowan a little extra too. 'We must get this recipe before we leave.'

'I'm not leaving,' Sasha said, snatching her plate back from her dad. 'I'm going to ask if I can stay. You and Mummy can go home without me and Tempest. But you can come and visit us a lot.'

'Well,' said Rowan, rolling her eyes in her usual fashion. 'That's the best news I've had all day.'

Chapter Five

Neva was in bed when Rafe finally returned. And she wasn't sure if he was pleased, or not, to find her there, because after a great deal of deliberation – and a phone call to Jo asking for advice – she had decided to go to his bed, not her own to wait for him.

She was still awake when he walked in, and she sat up in the huge four-poster bed ... and gave him the surprise of his life, it seemed.

His hand shot to his chest and he actually stumbled backwards when he saw her, illuminated solely by the glow from the fire still burning in the hearth. He immediately switched on the bedroom light.

'Dear God, Neva! For a moment I thought I might be seeing a ghost. Or having some other hallucination.'

'Don't ... don't you want me here?' He hadn't sounded annoyed, exactly, but neither did he seem happy to see her. 'I wanted to be here when you got home. I wanted to check you were OK. But if you'd rather, I'll go to my own room.'

She pushed back the covers and slid her legs over the side of the bed, revealing her reindeer and snowflake pyjamas.

'No.' He shook his head. He looked tired and sad. The complete opposite of how he had been just that morning. 'I'm sorry. I didn't mean it to sound like that.'

Neva switched on the bedside lamp as he turned off the light again and took off his jumper. He tossed it on a chair, slowly crossing the room towards her as if merely walking required all his strength.

'I'm glad you're here,' he continued. 'I'm just not used to having a gorgeous woman waiting for me in my bed, that's all.' He smiled and the sadness lifted from his face but his voice still held the intonation. 'Although I'm not sure I've got the energy to take advantage of the fact.'

'I'm not here because I want to have sex, Rafe.' She held out her hand to him and he took it and smiled again. 'Well I do, obviously. Especially after the last two nights.' She threw him a grin as he sat on the edge of the bed. 'But seriously. I'm here because I thought you might want a friendly smile. And perhaps, a cuddle.'

He looked her in the eye and, although he seemed surprised, his smile widened.

'A cuddle?' He nodded. 'Actually, yes. I think that's exactly what I need. And a kiss or two, perhaps.'

'As many as you want.' She wrapped her arms around him and kissed his cheek, his face and then his mouth and it was a minute or two before she spoke again. 'Are you OK?'

He was clearly distracted. Understandably so.

He shook his head. 'To be honest, Neva, I'm not sure how I feel.'

'Do you want to talk about it?'

He sighed softly. 'I would rather pretend none of it had happened, but it has. It's real and it's one hell of a mess. It's going to cause all sorts of changes. And gossip, of course. There'll be plenty of that.' He raked a hand through his hair and met her eye. 'Sorry. I'm not making much sense, am I?'

'That's fine. Just say whatever you want. Get it off your chest. Or not. I won't say anything unless you say you want me to. I don't know what's happened but I know it must be something big.'

'Oh it's big all right. It's huge. It's ... life-changing. And as Adam pointed out just after we arrived home, it's come at the worst time possible. Not that there was a good time for it once they'd all decided to keep the whole thing secret. But now we're just about to launch our Wyntersleap Gin, the last thing we needed was yet another family scandal.'

'A family scandal?' Neva swallowed the

lump that seemed to have formed in her throat. 'Does Adam have a child? Is that what this is about?'

'Does Adam what?' He looked her in the eye. 'Where did that come from? Has the gossip started already?'

'No.' Neva shook her head and kissed his cheek. 'That was me. I mean, I saw the way he looked at that stunning teenager at Amias Wells' house today and the way you both behaved after talking to her and I ... well, I just wondered. That's all.'

'And the first thought you had was that she was Adam's child?'

Neva lowered her eyes. 'Er. Or yours,' she mumbled.

'Mine?' He turned so abruptly that she almost toppled from the edge of the bed.

'Don't get cross. I didn't know what was going on. I still don't. I just...'

She should shut up. She would only make this worse if she carried on.

'You just assumed.'

'I jumped to conclusions. The wrong ones, no doubt. But look at it from my viewpoint, Rafe. You and Adam talk to a teenage girl. Then you both dash off back here and lock yourselves away with Olivia for hours, rowing, apparently and then she has a mild heart attack. What was I supposed to think? I'm sorry. But if people don't know what's going on, they'll automatically start making up scenarios of their own. Including me. I'm only human.'

He let out another sigh. 'You're right. I shouldn't snap at you. You're not to blame. In fact, you're the one bright light in all of this.'

He took both her hands in his and pulled her towards him, wrapping his arms tightly around her and hugging her close. So close that she was finding it hard to breathe. She tapped her fingers against his back and he loosened his grip just a little as he looked into her eyes.

'I love you, Rafe,' she said. 'Even though you did almost suffocate me.' She gave him a playful nudge. 'And I'll love you no matter what this is. Even if that stunning girl is your child, or it's something else entirely.'

He gave a little burst of laughter and kissed her forehead. 'She's not my child. Or Adam's. But she is our niece.'

'Your niece? Did you say, your niece? How come?'

He sighed once more and eased her from him but he took her hands in his again and met her look.

'You may have gathered from the things I told you just after we met that my mother and father didn't have a particularly good marriage. It seems it was even worse than I thought. It wasn't just my mother who had an affair. In fact, I'm not sure I blame her now for running off with that Count. I think, perhaps, my father drove her to it. Apparently, my father struggled with staying true to his marriage vows. He definitely had one affair, and possibly there were others, but the one that we now know of, produced a child. A child that he and Olivia, and also my mother, decided it was best if Adam and I knew absolutely nothing about.'

'Oh my God, Rafe! And you're saying that the teenage girl today was, sorry, is, the daughter of that child? But how could you tell? If you knew nothing of her existence, what made you and Adam so sure just by seeing her today? She doesn't look very much like either of you, or, from the portrait of your father I've seen, much like him. So how did Adam know just from her walking past him today? Because he did, didn't he? He knew right then.'

Rafe nodded. 'He had no idea she was so closely related. That was a shock to both of us. But we knew she was a relative. And one we had no knowledge of until today. And he knew it – we both knew it, because she has the Wynter birthmark.' He undid his shirt and slid it down before turning around.

'The holly leaf on your shoulder blade, you mean? That's a birthmark? A hereditary one? When I saw it on Christmas Eve, I thought that it was cute but I had no idea it was a birthmark. Are you saying Adam has one too?'

'Yes. Exactly the same as mine.'

'And the girl's is exactly the same too?'

36

'Yes. Her name is Kyra. Kyra Devon. And her mother's name is Catherine. And according to Kyra, Catherine has the same birthmark.'

'And Catherine is your sister? Your father's illegitimate child?'

'Yes. Although Adam and I didn't know that until Olivia told us. But we did know Kyra must be related to us in some way. She clearly had no idea who we were. It seems that Catherine doesn't know she is our sister. Or half-sister, to be precise, I suppose. Her mother also kept this fact from her, so Olivia told us. And I think, perhaps, this is the worst part of it all. The secret has been kept because Olivia paid Catherine's mother, Mary Devon and Mary Devon's mother, Viola Devon, to keep it. Olivia made them sign a contract in exchange for a certain sum of money. And as far as we are aware, the secret has remained until today, when Kyra strolled past Adam wearing a T-shirt revealing the Wynter birthmark. Every Wynter has it, and has had for generations.'

'Olivia paid them? What about your dad? Didn't he have a say in the matter?'

'It seems he had very little to say about it at the time. Then Mother left, and not long after, he died, so we'll never know if he would've kept the secret or if, one day, he would've told Adam and I that we had another sibling.'

'But how do you know your sister doesn't

know about you and Adam?'

He shrugged. 'Olivia says there is no way that Mary or Viola Devon would've told Catherine. Olivia threatened them with lawsuits if they ever revealed the fact. She even asked them to spread rumours that the child may be someone else's, which, apparently, they did. And that too, was a bit of a shock. The person who some people believed to be Catherine's biological father is actually the father of a friend of ours – Amias Wells. The man whose house we were at today. Mary Devon had once dated Alwick Wells, Amias' father, and despite the fact that he was married at the time of Mary's pregnancy, she and Viola Devon hinted that the baby might be his.'

'Oh my God, Rafe! That's awful. Is that why Olivia had a heart attack? The shock of you and Adam discovering the family secret was too much for her?'

He shook his head as he threw off his shirt and tossed that on the chair with his jumper.

'She would certainly rather we hadn't found out. Neither Catherine nor Kyra live around here, so I think Olivia was hoping it was a secret she would take to her grave. But our confronting her about it wasn't what caused the heart attack. As far as she is concerned, she acted in the best interests of the Wynters and clearly doesn't regret it, or any part she played. The only regret she has is that we found out.

You won't believe this, but she actually said that she had asked Mary Devon to give the baby up. Her intention was to then put the baby up for adoption in the hope that none of us would ever see the child again. Those were her exact words. She really is unbelievable at times.'

He shook his head again and sighed as his entire body seemed to slump deeper into the bed.

Neva took one of his hands in hers and squeezed it, hoping to give him some comfort.

'She does seem to feel very strongly about your family name. But if it wasn't the shock of you and Adam finding out, what did cause her heart attack?'

He ran his free hand through his hair and met her eyes.

'It was what I threatened I'd do if she didn't change her ways.'

'Change her ways? What else has she done then?'

'What else?' He looked bemused as his brows knit together. 'She's treated you appallingly since the moment you arrived. And if anything, that has only got worse since Christmas Eve when it became apparent I'd fallen in love with you. The way she behaved towards you during dinner yesterday was frankly unforgivable. I was prepared to overlook it, given her age, the shock of having so many people living under this roof at such short notice, and me divulging my new business venture. I thought she just needed some time to come to terms with all the changes. But discovering that she's kept our sister from us, and would've done so for our entire lives if she could, was the final straw. I said things she found dreadfully upsetting.'

'What did you threaten to do? It can't have been that bad because although I've only known you for a few days, I know in my heart you're not a cruel, mean or hurtful man.'

He gave her a quick smile. 'Thank you for your belief in me. But I was cruel. I threatened to send her to live in the village.'

Neva waited for him to continue but he didn't. He lowered his head as if ashamed.

'And?'

'And?' He met her questioning look. 'Believe me, Neva. That was all it took to give her a heart attack. Although the doctor told us that the shock alone wouldn't have done that. There would have already been a problem with her heart or arteries, and that's one of the things the tests will show.'

A burst of laughter escaped Neva's lips but she quickly suppressed it.

'I must be missing something. Are you honestly telling me that you thought that threatening to send her to live in the village gave her a heart attack? I know lots of people who would give anything to live in the village.

Although not at the moment, that's true. Is that what she thought you meant? You'd send her to a flooded village? She knows you wouldn't do that.'

'No, Neva. You don't understand. To Olivia, being sent to live in the village, even at its best, is tantamount to being exiled. Olivia is a Wynter. Not by birth, that's true, but by marriage. All Wynters see Wynter House as their home. Even if, like Adam, they choose to live elsewhere. Although he does return here most weekends and holidays. But Wynter House is still his home, as it is for all Wynters. To be cast out of the house and sent to live in a cottage in the village is a monumental and exceedingly shameful event.'

'That's ridiculous. And rather snooty and rude, to be honest.'

'Welcome to my world.'

'Is that how you feel, Rafe? Do you think the Wynters are all far too high and mighty to live in the village?'

'Er. We're not high and mighty. But we do belong at Wynter House.'

'And me, Rafe? Where does someone like me belong? Olivia's made it very clear she thinks I'm nowhere near good enough to lick your boots, let alone anything else. Do you think you're lowering your standards by dating me?'

'What? No. Where did that come from?

You're forgetting I married a barmaid. Much to Olivia's consternation.'

'Ah yes, Pippa. Is that what this is about? Do you do this on purpose to annoy Olivia? Do you date women like Pippa and me to show her you don't care what she thinks?'

'Women like you and Pippa? You and Pippa are as different as it's possible to be.'

'But we're not from your world, are we? A barmaid and a hairdresser. Is that a coincidence or a pattern?'

'I don't understand. If you're actually suggesting that I'm with you to annoy Olivia then I really am crap at showing my true feelings. And it's hardly a pattern, is it? I fell in love with Pippa over nineteen years ago and it's been more than fourteen since we divorced. Between then and now, I may have only dated a few women, but they've come from a variety of backgrounds. I didn't fall in love with you because you were a hairdresser, Neva. That's ludicrous. And I didn't want to fall in love with you. Or anyone for that matter, at the moment. It just happened. But I'm overjoyed it has. I would've fallen for you no matter what you did for a living. Where is this coming from? And how did we go from discussing Olivia and the discovery of my sister, to why I fell in love with you? I'm confused. I'm also very tired. I really need some sleep. Can we discuss this in the morning? I love you, Neva. Surely that's enough? Do I have to try to explain why?'

'No. I'm sorry. I'm being ridiculous. You're right. I'm accusing you of thinking I'm not good enough for you when the truth is, that's what's going through my own mind. I'm being silly and selfish and I apologise. But I can't help it. I even told my best friend, Jo today that I was terrified you might dump me.'

'Dump you!' He pulled her to him. 'There's no chance of that happening, I can promise you.' He grinned suddenly. 'I'd rather go and live in the village than lose you. If anyone runs a risk of being dumped, it's me. Especially with my family history to contend with. And now I have relatives I didn't even know existed. Let's pray to God they don't take after Olivia.'

'What are you going to do? About the new relatives, I mean. Are you going to contact them? You said they didn't live around here. Does that mean they're visiting someone who does? Do Mary and Viola Devon live somewhere close by?'

Mary and Viola live in Merriment Bay, and always have, according to Olivia. I've probably met them or seen them around because it's not a large place, is it? But that's what makes this whole thing even more extraordinary. While we were at the hospital this evening, discussing Olivia's prognosis with one of the doctors – who is actually a friend of Adam's, the doctor was called away. When she returned, sometime later, she apologised for keeping us waiting. She wouldn't normally have discussed other patients, but being Adam's friend, she did. You know how charming Adam can be. What she told us knocked us for six. She said there had been two deaths tonight. One was an elderly woman who'd had a fall and been in a coma for weeks and the other was an elderly friend of the woman's, who'd come all the way from Canada to see her. They both died of heart failure and both within half an hour or so of one another. She said that the woman lived in Merriment Bay and she thought we might know her as Adam and I both have several friends there. And this is the strangest part of all. The woman was Viola Devon. My half-sister's grandmother. So now we really don't know what to do. It's hardly the time to go and introduce ourselves to Catherine, is it?'

'Wow! Really? Bloody hell. What a truly strange coincidence! Er. No. I suppose it isn't the best time then. But then again, perhaps it is. Catherine may have lost one relative, but she'll gain an entirely new family in you, Adam and Olivia.'

'Yes. But perhaps she would rather not.'

Having met Olivia, Neva would probably advise towards the 'not'. But she wasn't going to say that to Rafe. Besides, Rafe and Adam were definitely worth meeting.

'Oh I don't know. I'm very, very pleased I

met you. And I'd be happy to discover I had you and Adam for brothers. Although I'm glad you're not my brother, of course. Because if you were, I couldn't kiss you like this.'

She kissed him on the lips and gently pushed him onto his back, kissing him all the while.

He grinned at her when she eased away from him.

'I'm also glad I'm not your brother. And suddenly, I don't feel so tired, after all.'

He kicked off his shoes and pulled her back into his arms.

Chapter Six

Only Neva, Rafe and Adam knew the reason for Olivia's heart attack, but as Neva and Rafe walked into the dining room for breakfast the following day, it was obvious that both she and Rafe had been right about the gossip. Adam was directly behind them and it was clear by the sudden silence, followed by one or two embarrassed mumbles, that all the guests at Wynter House had been discussing the topic.

'I think we're going to have to tell them something,' Rafe said, in a low voice as Adam came and stood beside him. 'I've told Neva, obviously.'

Adam glanced at Neva before turning his attention back to Rafe. 'Of course you have. But what would you say? Something like, "We have news. We've got a sister and a niece and it almost killed Olivia to tell us about them." Do we really want everybody knowing about this before we've had a chance to discuss it properly? We need to decide what we're going to do, Rafe, preferably before we make it public knowledge. So I'd appreciate it, Neva, if you wouldn't mention this to your family just yet.'

'OK. I won't say a word.'

Rafe looked at Adam. 'More secrets? Haven't we had enough of those?'

Adam raised his brows. 'Says the man who kept his new business a secret for more than eighteen months ... Morning everyone.' He smiled at Rafe and marched purposefully towards the dining table. 'You'll be pleased to hear that Olivia is doing well and we expect her to make a full recovery and return to Wynter House within a few days. Don't we, Rafe?'

Rafe squeezed Neva's hand and softly sighed. 'Yes. A complete recovery.'

'What caused it?' Cecil asked, nonchalantly spreading honey on a slice of toast. 'It was a mild heart attack, we heard.'

'Olivia's not as young as we like to think she is,' Adam said, taking a seat beside Sasha. 'These things happen at her age. While we were at the hospital last night, two other elderly people passed away. It was sad, but actually quite romantic. They had been friends and one had travelled thousands of miles to see the other. They died within thirty minutes of each other. We were lucky Olivia didn't make it three. With a few minor changes to her diet and a little bit of extra care, Olivia will be back to her old self in no time.'

'Does that mean Neva can't marry Rafe?'

Sasha asked.

'Sasha!' Neva glowered at her niece as she took the chair next to Rowan.

Rafe looked surprised, but he smiled. 'It doesn't mean any such thing.'

'What?' Adam shot a look at Rafe and Neva who were now sitting opposite him and he shook his head but he was grinning. 'You've only been a couple for three days. That's a bit quick even for you, Rafe.'

'We're not getting married.' Neva hadn't meant to shriek. 'Er. What I meant was, you're right, Adam. It has only been a few days. We haven't even talked about what happens in the New Year, let alone that far ahead.'

Sasha frowned. 'But yesterday you said–'

'I said you shouldn't repeat things you think you hear, sweetie.'

Neva threw Sasha a warning look and thankfully, Sasha didn't continue but Rafe looked at them both and there was a hint of a question in his eyes, as if he was asking if Neva was having doubts about spending the future with him. If he had concerns, he didn't voice them.

'This holiday has certainly been full of surprises,' Rowan said. 'Oh, and speaking of surprises, Rafe, Sasha is going to ask you, yet again, if she and Tempest can live here. I want you to know, it's fine with us.' She leant forward and grinned and winked at him and

Neva.

'Yes, yes, yes.' Sasha bounced up and down in her chair. 'And Mummy and Daddy will come and stay every weekend. And Granny and Gramps, too.'

Neva knew Rowan was joking, but was it really wise to let Sasha believe that staying on at Wynter House was a possibility? Someone would eventually have to tell the child that she would be going home with her mum and dad. And that wasn't going to be Neva. Or Rafe.

Perhaps Rowan was simply delaying the inevitable temper tantrums until the day they all left. They'd booked the cottage in the village until Friday the 3rd of January and although no departure date had been discussed since they had all decamped to Wynter House and Rafe had said they could stay, Neva and her family had assumed they would still be leaving on or around that date.

Rowan and Nigel had the family business of Grey Building & Design to get back to. And since Dawn and Dennis had handed it over to them as a Christmas present, they'd have a lot to do and wouldn't want to delay any longer.

Dawn and Dennis had to get home and make their final preparations for their move from Surrey to their new house in Merriment Bay. Completion of their sale was set for the 8th of January, just two days before Neva and Jo's completion date for the sale of their own

London flat.

None of the Greys could stay beyond the original, planned departure date. And that included Sasha, whether she liked it or not. Maybe they could say that Olivia said Sasha had to go. That way none of them would be 'the bad guy'. Not even Sasha would be able to argue with Olivia Wynter.

'Thank you for letting me know,' Rafe said, grinning first at Neva and Rowan and then at Sasha, opposite, and obviously happy to go along with the joke. 'But I hope you realise, Sasha, that you'll have to work if you stay. Everybody who lives here, has to. Apart from Olivia, because she's far too old to work.'

Sasha frowned. 'And I'm too young. I'm only eight. It's the law. Mummy says that I should be glad I live in England because if I lived in India or somewhere, I'd have to make clothes, but the law here says I can't.' She beamed at him. 'But I'll get rid of all your ghosts. And if Olivia dies, I'll get rid of her too.'

'That'll please her,' Adam said, a snort of laughter escaping as he poured Neva, Rafe and himself some coffee from a large pot on the table. 'I'll be sure to mention it when Rafe and I visit her today.'

'I'm so sorry,' Rowan said, now glaring at Sasha. 'I don't know why these dreadful things just tumble out of her mouth. We didn't bring her up to be rude and unfeeling.'

'It's not a problem,' Rafe said. 'She's young. She doesn't understand.'

Neva tutted. 'She understands a lot more than you might imagine.' She lowered her voice. 'Which reminds me, Rowan. You might want to take up Judith's original offer of Sasha having a room of her own. Unless you want everyone at Wynter House to hear about your sex life.'

'What?' Rowan shot a look at Sasha who was now busy concentrating on cutting her toast into ghost shapes before slicing off the ghosts' heads. 'I'll kill her if she does.'

'She told me you and Nigel rowed about sex on Christmas morning but that you had sex on Christmas night because she heard you.'

'Oh my God!' Rowan blushed profusely before coughing and glancing down the table. 'Judith? When you have a moment, may I have a quick word with you please?'

'Of course. We can have a chat right after breakfast. Oh. Unless you want to speak to me first, Rafe? Do you need me to do anything for you this morning? Or before you and Adam go to the hospital today?'

Rafe shook his head. 'No. Although I'll give the hospital a call and see if Olivia is asking for anything and if so, I'll let you know.'

'I can call the hospital,' Judith offered. 'Unless you'd rather do so.'

'Thanks, Judith, but I think it's best if

Adam or I call. Just in case.'

'I'll do it,' Adam said. 'Don't you and Sean have to discuss your new business? I thought the plan was to get that up and running without further delay now you've perfected your first batch.'

Having broken the news to Olivia about the gin distillery on Christmas Eve, and shown it to Neva on Christmas Day, Rafe and Sean's 'Wyntersleep Gin' was now no secret. They had told all the guests and staff at Wynter House about it over cocktails on Christmas Day – after the eyeball sweets incident, and Sasha being sent to bed. Everyone had tasted the gin and given their genuine approval. Even Cecil and Ronnie had only good things to say about it.

'It is,' Sean said. 'And more so as I've no idea how long it'll be until Wyntersleep Inn's open for business again. We'll have to find another outlet for it in the meantime.'

'Weren't you intending to do that anyway?' Neva asked.

'Yes.' Rafe nodded. 'But we were hoping to have a soft launch at the Inn and then a week or two later, invite some press and potential buyers. The plan was to serve them lunch, get them to try the gin and then bring them here, via Wyntersleep Falls, for a tour of the distillery. We were intending to serve afternoon tea, followed by the tour and return here for cocktails. But that was before the village flooded. And now with Olivia's health in question...' He shook his head as his voice trailed off.

'You had a soft launch on Christmas Day,' Nigel said, smiling at Rafe. 'We all loved it. Couldn't you go straight to the next phase based on that?'

Rafe glanced at Adam and Sean. 'I suppose so. What do you think?'

Adam nodded in agreement as Sean looked at Wendy and they both nodded.

'I guess we could,' Sean said. 'There were probably more people trying it here on Christmas Day than we would've got at the Inn in any event. And Nigel is right. No one had a bad word to say about it.'

Neva nodded too. 'And this house is so large, does Olivia's health really cause an issue as far as launching your gin is concerned? I realise you're worried about her but if she's in her own suite of rooms, she probably wouldn't even know any of the press and the buyers were here.'

'That's true,' Adam agreed.

'You could have lunch here,' Penny suggested. 'Taryn, Wendy and I could organise that without too much upheaval for all your current guests. We could have two separate lunch sittings. One for everyone already here and another for the press and your buyers.'

'If the water's receded completely and the

meltwater from the snow isn't an issue,' Gavin said, 'we could drive them to the village and back in our various cars. They'd still have to walk a short way to the Falls but we could drop them all close by.'

Adam smiled. 'That sounds like a good plan. I'm happy to play chauffeur for the day, even if it's during the week. I can take a few days off. And something's just occurred to me. Do you remember Amelia Goodbody, Rafe? She's in marketing, I believe. I could get her to pop down and give us a few tips. I'm sure she'd do it for free. Or at least in exchange for a few nights here. She came with some of my other friends this summer, for the weekend of the annual Wyntersleap cricket match and she said then that she'd love to come back and stay.'

Rafe furrowed his brows. 'Amelia Goodbody? The name rings a bell but I can't say I remember her. That would be very helpful. Assuming she would be willing to do that.'

'Amelia Goodbody?' Neva repeated. 'Does she live up to her name?'

'Amelia?' Adam teased. 'Or the Goodbody part? Because she definitely lives up to that. In fact, it should be hyphenated. Amelia Very-Goodbody, from what I recall.'

'I thought you said she's a friend of yours,' Gavin said, grinning. 'And yet you only "recall" her having a good body?'

Adam grinned back. 'She's not a close friend. She was actually dating another friend of mine. But I heard a few weeks ago that it was over. The more I think about it, the more I'm convinced it's a good idea to invite her to stay. And not merely to help you out with your new business, Rafe.'

Chapter Seven

Rafe and Adam said nothing to anyone except Neva, about Catherine and Kyra Devon. The fact that Catherine was their sibling was going to remain a secret until Olivia had recovered and was back at Wynter House.

'Once Olivia is home,' Rafe said, when he and Neva were in his bed that night, 'we'll discuss what to do. Adam and I both want to meet Catherine, and to explain to Kyra why we acted so strangely on Boxing Day, but it can wait. When we were at the hospital today, we heard from another of Adam's friends, that Viola Devon's funeral isn't until the end of the first week of January. We're thinking that it might be best to leave it until after then to contact Catherine.'

Neva snuggled against Rafe and looked up into his eyes.

'Adam seems to have a lot of friends.'

'He does. He's a very friendly person.'

'Hmm. I bet this other friend was a woman, wasn't she?'

Rafe furrowed his brows and met her look.

'As it happens, yes. But he does have several male friends, too. He's always been good with people. Far more so than I.'

'Oh I don't know.' Neva kissed him on his neck and trailed a finger across his broad chest. 'I can think of one person you're very good with.'

'Oh? Who?' He grinned at her and winked before kissing her briefly on the lips. 'Let's hope it stays that way and you don't start thinking you fell in love with the wrong Wynter brother.'

'No chance of that.'

She smiled at him and kissed him in return.

He twisted a length of her hair around his fingers.

'When you first came to stay, I thought it was Adam you were interested in. Not me.'

She looked him directly in the eye and sighed.

'In the interest of totally honest, Rafe, and not keeping secrets. It was. But only at first and only for a moment. Like you, I didn't want a relationship and I certainly didn't want to fall in love. Well. Not yet, anyway. I thought Adam was handsome and fun, and that there might be a chance we could have a quick fling. Don't get cross.'

'I'm not. He is handsome and fun and most women think so.'

'I can feel you tensing up and there's really no reason to. I think I fell in love with you almost as soon as we met. You certainly irritated me and as much as I tried not to, it was you I kept thinking about, Rafe. Not Adam. That's the complete and utter truth. Even if you hadn't fallen for me, I wouldn't have had a fling with Adam after getting to know you. I would've sat and pined for you instead. I love you, Rafe. Adam doesn't interest me at all. Not in that way, at least.'

He smiled. 'I'm very glad to hear it. I've never been jealous of Adam before. But when I thought it was him you wanted, I was eaten up with jealousy. It wasn't a pleasant feeling. And it's not something I'd experienced. Not even when Pippa had her affair. I didn't feel jealous of her lover. Just disappointed in her and heartbroken that our marriage was over.' He slid his hand from her hair and gave her a serious look. 'Promise me one thing, Neva. If you do fall out of love with me, or in love with someone else, please tell me right away. I don't want there to be any secrets between us. Ever.'

She ran her finger over his lips and shook her head.

'I will promise you that. Even though there's no need. I know in my heart there'll never be anyone for me now, other than you, Rafe. And will you promise me the same?'

He smiled and visibly relaxed. 'I will. But

there's no need. You're the only woman for me, Neva. There'll never be anyone else but you.'

'I hope Olivia doesn't have another heart attack when you break that news to her.'

He grinned but was soon serious again. 'I need to ask you something else.'

'Ask me anything you want.'

He gave a small cough. 'Why did you seem so shocked when Sasha mentioned us getting married? I know it's early days, but if we both love one another as much as we do, isn't that the natural conclusion?'

She looked him in the eye as her heart skipped a beat and her tummy did a somersault.

'I hope so. Yes. I just didn't want you to think that I'd assumed we would. Or that I'd said anything to anyone about it. Because, despite how we feel, it is too soon to think about that. Isn't it?'

His brows knit together for a second. 'Is it? I don't know. If someone had asked me two weeks ago, I'd have said I'll never get married again. Now. I can't imagine not being with you. Not having you in my life. I can't imagine my future without you in it.'

'You're tensing again. I can feel it.' She pushed herself away from him and tried to sit up. 'Are you already having doubts? Or does that thought simply frighten you?'

He smiled and pulled her back towards

him.

'I'm not having doubts about you, Neva. Or about us. Absolutely not. Talking of the future made me think about Catherine and Kyra again. Catherine's the same age as Adam and Kyra's eighteen. We've missed so much of one another's lives. But once we meet, both Catherine and Kyra will be part of our future. They're Wynters. Yet I know nothing about them. Catherine is my sister and Kyra is my niece. That does frighten me.'

'I can understand that. But I'm sure it'll be fine and once you do meet, you'll probably soon find you have lots of things in common. Just thank your lucky stars that Kyra's eighteen and not eight. And that she's nothing like my incorrigible niece.'

He laughed suddenly. 'Sasha is wonderful. I've grown very fond of her. Even Archie has a soft spot for her.'

'What? A muddy hole in the garden, you mean?'

'No. I'm serious. He is fond of her. But don't tell him I told you that. He'll never forgive me.'

'My lips are sealed.' She had a sudden thought. 'Um. You said earlier that Viola Devon's funeral is in early January. Will Catherine and Kyra be returning to wherever it is they live after that? If so, you may not have much time to meet them.'

'No. We thought she and Kyra were in Merriment Bay on a visit, but it seems, from what Adam's friend said today, that they've been in the village since mid-August and will be staying for the foreseeable future, so there's really no rush. I have no idea what we're going to say to them. We can't simply knock on the door and introduce ourselves. Or invite them here for afternoon tea, can we?'

'Not for afternoon tea with everyone else. No. But afternoon tea for just you and Adam and Catherine and Kyra might be a pleasant way to break the ice. Penny and Taryn do make the most delicious cakes. Although Carruthers can be a bit intimidating. Until you get to know him. And actually, so can you. Remember to smile and not look all moody and grouchy like you did when we first met.'

'Moody and grouchy? Me?' He gave her a hurt look but was clearly teasing. 'Well I had just dived into a freezing and rather wild river in the torrential rain to save a runaway puppy.'

'True. Actually. I think I fell a little bit in love with you right then. Not just because you saved Tempest but because after you did, and you were lying on the bank with Tempest sprawled beside you, you patted her reassuringly as if to tell her she was safe. It brought a tear to my eye. And it showed what a kind and tender man you really are.'

'And then you shouted at me.' He laughed

again and shook his head.

'You shouted at me first. I wanted to slap you after that.'

'I could see that from the expression on your face. I was furious at the time. But even then, I wanted to kiss you.'

'What?'

He nodded. 'It's true. That's what annoyed me the most. I saw you as I walked back up that bank and I had an immediate and completely ludicrous urge to kiss you.'

'You did? Really? But you were rude and arrogant and marched off after giving me a lecture. Did you really want to kiss me?'

'Yes. Although I had no idea why. Perhaps it was simply because I was glad that both the puppy and I had got out of that river alive.' He grinned devilishly and pulled her closer to him. 'And I seem to have a similar urge right now. But I want to do a great deal more than kiss you.'

He wrapped his arms around her and kissed her passionately and as far as Neva was concerned, all further discussions about Catherine and Kyra and everything else could definitely wait until the morning.

Chapter Eight

Neva didn't like keeping a secret from her family, or from her best friend, Jo, but it wasn't her secret and she wouldn't betray Rafe's trust. Or Adam's.

'But I won't tell anyone,' Jo grumbled, when Neva wouldn't 'spill'.

'That's not the point, Jo. Rafe and Adam have asked me not to tell anyone yet and I promised I wouldn't. You know I'd tell you if I could. But revealing it would hurt Rafe, if he ever found out, and I'm not prepared to do that. I'll tell you as soon as I can.'

'OK. Fine. But you know I'll still keep asking.'

And she asked again the following day.

'I still can't tell you. How are things going there?'

'I'm not going to tell you,' Jo said, in a petulant voice, before laughing. 'I don't know why I'm laughing. It's bloody miserable here. I still need to talk to Rob once his family leaves, but with every passing day, I feel more and more certain that this relationship is over and that, assuming your offer is still open, I'll be moving with you to Merriment Bay.'

'I'm sorry, Jo. And yes, the offer is still open. You know that. Even if you decide to wait and give things more time, you'll be welcome in Merriment Bay whenever you want to come.'

'Aw, thank you. I love you for that. I love you anyway.'

'I love you too.'

'It's pretty grim though, when the highlight of my day is talking to you and hearing about what's happening at Wynter House. Any news about Olivia? Or is that a secret too?'

Neva tutted. 'The doctors said Olivia could return home today, so she must be OK. She's only been in hospital for a few days and her test results were good, apparently. Adam said the other day that the doctors are certain that with a little extra care and a few lifestyle changes, she'll make a complete recovery. We were all expecting Rafe to call from the hospital this afternoon and say they were on their way. But Olivia informed them and the doctors that she didn't feel quite right, so further tests are being carried out. Rafe is concerned, but Adam isn't.'

'Sounds like she may be milking it.'

'I was wondering that myself. But I haven't said that to Rafe. We'll have to wait and see what happens.'

Adam seemed even less concerned the

following day.

'I think she wants to punish us,' he said, as they sat down for breakfast, the day before New Year's Eve. 'She knows how guilty Rafe feels and she's making the most of the situation. She's in a private room and is being waited on hand and foot, so it's basically a home-from-home.'

'Would she really do that? Punish you both, I mean.'

Neva hated hospitals and couldn't wait to get out of them, so she couldn't imagine anyone wanting to stay in one unless it was absolutely necessary. Although she had been wondering about Olivia.

'I wouldn't put anything past her. I assume Rafe's told you he's going to hire a live-in nurse to come and take care of her once she does come home.'

'Yes. He said one of the doctors is a friend of yours and has recommended someone from a private nursing agency.'

Adam nodded. 'Olivia's already told us exactly what she thinks of that. It was nothing good. But she's rather shot herself in the foot by pretending she's still unwell. She miraculously felt better by the time we left yesterday evening, and says she wants to come home today.'

'Perhaps that's what Rafe's discussing right now. The hospital called him as we were coming in for breakfast.'

As if on cue, Rafe came and joined them, an anxious expression on his face.

'Olivia won't be coming home today. There's an outbreak of the Norovirus at the hospital and she's been sick and had diarrhoea for most of the night. They're reducing visiting hours and restricting it to close family only.'

A sardonic smile crept across Adam's face. 'I bet she's wishing she'd come home when the doctors originally said she could. So she won't be here for New Year's Eve?'

Rafe sat beside Neva and shook his head. 'She won't be home until at least the end of the week, most likely. Or possibly the weekend.'

'We won't get to say goodbye then,' Neva said, uncertain whether this fact pleased her or not. 'We're leaving on Friday.'

Rafe looked surprised. 'Are you? Why?'

Neva grinned at him. 'Because that's the end of our holiday.'

'But that doesn't mean you have to go. You can stay for as long as you want. I ... I'd assumed you would be.'

'Staying?'

He nodded. 'Yes.'

She met the look in his eyes. 'I'd love to, Rafe. But my flat's being sold and I need to go back to London to pack up my things. Damn. I've just realised. I forgot to book a removal van. I was going to sort all that stuff out during this holiday, but what with everything else, that didn't happen. I must try to do that today. We're moving out on the 10th and that's less than two weeks away.'

'You're moving to Merriment Bay that day?' Adam asked. 'I hadn't realised the purchase of your flat and salon was that far advanced.'

'It isn't. Although the owner does want a quick sale and Dad set everything in motion the day before Christmas Eve, when you took us all to Merriment Bay. Horton & Wells, estate agents are dealing with the sale and they sent the details to Lester & Young solicitors that day, so it shouldn't be long.'

'They're all friends of ours,' Rafe said.

'Yes.' Adam nodded. 'Perhaps we could see if there's anything Natalia and Josh Horton, and Will Lester can do to speed things up.'

'That would be brilliant. Thanks. Dad's hoping we can exchange contracts this week and have a quick completion. The plan was for me to stay with Mum and Dad at their new home until then and put my things in their garage. To be honest, I don't have that much to bring. Jo and I bought the cheapest furniture we could when we bought the flat and although we kept saying we'd replace it, we never did. After ten years, most of it's falling apart. I'm only planning to move my bedroom furniture, one chair that I love, a side table and my books and other personal stuff.'

'You could keep that here,' Rafe offered. 'Your parents might still be in a bit of a mess themselves having just moved a couple of days before you. We've got room and as it happens, we know a guy who owns a local removal firm. I'll give him a call and see if he's free. You could move your things whenever you like, if he is. You don't have to wait until your actual completion date. And you can stay here.'

'That would be wonderful, Rafe. And it's very kind of you, but the thing is, it may not just be me.'

'Oh?' Adam looked surprised.

Rafe grinned at Adam. 'Neva means her best friend Jo may be moving down to Merriment Bay with her.' He beamed at Neva. 'She's welcome to stay too. One more person won't make much difference. And as Rowan, Nigel and Sasha, and your mum and dad will have left, there'll be plenty of empty rooms. In fact, I can't wait to meet her in person, having spoken to her on the phone yesterday.'

Adam raised his brows. 'Your best friend? I assume from what you said, she's single.'

'Strictly speaking, no. She's just got engaged and moved in with her fiancé. That's why we sold the flat we jointly own in London. But she's decided it was all a big mistake and it seems pretty certain that she's going to be living with me in the flat in Merriment Bay and helping me run the new business.'

Adam grinned mischievously. 'Is she as pretty as you?'

Rafe tutted. 'Please don't flirt with my girlfriend.'

Neva laughed. 'She's prettier. And she's great fun too. I'm hoping Rafe won't think he's got second best.'

'Never.' Rafe pulled her to him and kissed her.

Adam's grin broadened. 'Rafe's right. You should both definitely stay here with us until your new flat completes. I rather like the sound of Jo.'

Chapter Nine

Unfortunately for almost everyone at Wynter House, Olivia wasn't the only one who had contracted the Norovirus. Judith, who had visited the hospital with Rafe and Adam, at Olivia's request, the previous day was the first to show signs of it. Her symptoms began shortly after breakfast.

'You don't look well, Judith,' Neva said.

She, Dawn, Rowan and even Sasha were helping Penny, Taryn and Judith clear the table.

'I do feel a little unwell.'

Judith suddenly bent almost double, grabbing her stomach and screwing up her face in pain. A second or two later, she threw up.

'She's been bitten by a Zombie!' Sasha yelled, taking photos on her phone.

'Stop that right now.' Rowan took the phone away and slipped it in the pocket of her jeans.

'Sit down,' Neva said. 'I'll go and get Rafe and Carruthers.'

'No,' Judith moaned. 'Please don't trouble them. I'll be fine.'

'I'll get a bowl.' Taryn dashed off in the direction of the kitchen.

'Drink some water.' Penny handed Judith the glass she had just filled.

'Oh good gracious.' Judith paled visibly and held her stomach again. 'I think I need to get to the bathroom fairly quickly.'

'I'll help you,' Penny linked her arm through Judith's. 'I think she may have the Norovirus. Best if you all stay away. I'll get her to the bathroom and then up to her room. You had better tell Rafe and Carruthers after all.'

Penny was right and it wasn't long before nearly everyone succumbed to the virus. Most of them fell ill later that day, including Rowan, but Neva and Nigel seemed fine until the following morning. Sadly, that was New Year's Eve, so the day and evening didn't quite go as anyone had expected. The celebratory dinner was cancelled and replaced with chicken broth, which none of them could bring themselves to eat. The champagne remained unopened and Wynter House was the quietest it had ever been as the antique clocks in several of the rooms, chimed out the old year and rang in the new.

Only Sasha and Rafe escaped the clutches of the virus. Rafe nursed them all, including Carruthers, back to health, which thankfully, didn't take too long. Ethel was unwell for longer than most and at one point, Rafe told Neva he was so concerned he had called a doctor, but when he told Ethel, she refused to go to hospital.

'What's the point? I'd rather be sick here than there. And if I'm going to die anywhere, I don't want it to be in a hospital.'

She smacked her toothless gums together and refused to discuss the matter further.

Rafe gave in when the doctor assured him Ethel would pull through and was already on the mend.

Sasha retrieved her phone from Rowan's discarded jeans about half an hour after Rowan took to her bed, and took photos of anyone who was foolish enough to let her into their rooms. She posted the pictures on Rowan's social media accounts with various hashtags ranging from hashtag slimy sick to hashtag zombie apocalypse.

Sasha had to ask Rafe how to spell apocalypse and Rowan was less than pleased that he had told her. Rowan also bitterly regretted letting Sasha ever find out her social media passwords, and vowed to change them the moment she felt well enough. And to throttle her daughter while she was at it.

Neva was upset to miss New Year's Eve. She had been looking forward to the celebrations and to toasting in the New Year in Rafe's arms. She did spend the evening in his arms. But she had her head over a sick bowl at the time.

'The man is clearly besotted,' Jo said, when she called Neva on New Year's Day to wish her a happy 2020. 'Any man who holds your hair back while you're throwing up, is absolutely head over heels in love. And is definitely a keeper.'

'It wasn't the romantic evening I'd hoped for though.'

'But it proves beyond a shadow of a doubt that he's a really good guy and that he's nuts about you. That counts for something. And you'll have every New Year from here on in to celebrate with him. I'm looking forward to meeting him.'

'And he's looking forward to meeting you. Oh, and he's said we can both stay here when we move out of the flat. But we'll talk about that later. I think I'm going to be sick again.'

'Happy New Year,' Jo said. 'I'll call you later.'

Chapter Ten

Olivia was finally well enough to return to Wynter House on Friday 3rd of January –the same day the Greys were due to leave and despite the fact that Dawn and Dennis and Rowan and Nigel were still a little drained from the sickness, they decided to stick with their plans and go home to Surrey.

'We still have things to do to prepare for our move,' Dawn said. 'But we'll take it easy until we're feeling one hundred per cent.'

'And we need to get home to re-open the business on Monday,' Rowan added. 'The weekend will give us time to rest and relax in readiness for that.'

'I want to stay,' Sasha said, sticking out her bottom lip and crossing her arms sulkily.

'Mummy and Daddy need your help,' Neva told her. Adding in a whisper, 'And Olivia Wynter has said she wants the house to herself, so we've all got to go today.'

She didn't tell Sasha that she wouldn't be leaving until after the weekend, Rafe having suggested she stay on for at least another couple of days.

'But Ethel and Queenie are staying,' Sasha said. 'And so is everyone else from the village.'

'Yes. But Olivia knows them all and even she wouldn't send them back to flooded cottages. Our homes aren't flooded. We have no reason to stay. And if you go home now, Rafe said you can come back and stay very soon. Possibly during half-term. That's something to look forward to, isn't it?'

Sasha didn't look convinced, but when Rafe later assured her that she was welcome back at any time, she finally agreed to go.

'Thank you so much for everything, Rafe,' Dawn said, as they were about to leave. 'This has been a Christmas and New Year we'll never forget.'

'You're welcome here whenever you want to visit,' he said.

'And you're welcome to come and visit us in our new home,' Dennis said.

Rowan thanked Rafe profusely, especially for putting up with Sasha and Tempest, and for saving Tempest's life.

'Who knew that day you jumped into the river to save our puppy that you'd soon be in love with my sister? This has certainly been an eventful holiday. Thanks again for everything. And you're welcome to visit us in Surrey, too.'

Rafe smiled and glanced lovingly at Neva.

'I still can't quite believe that Neva loves me. But I'm very pleased things turned out the way they did.'

Everyone, apart from Ethel who was still a little weak, came out to say their goodbyes to Dawn, Dennis, Rowan, Nigel and Sasha and Tempest and it took at least half an hour before the Greys were finally on their way. Those remaining were standing on the parking area of the drive, now completely clear of snow thanks to a spell of mild weather, waving them off, as Olivia arrived home in a private ambulance. Neva couldn't help but smile as they all dashed back inside at the sight of it.

'I think I'll join them,' she said, smiling up at Rafe. 'Olivia may have another heart attack if she discovers I'm still here.'

Rafe didn't try to stop her. 'She'll have to get used to the idea. But perhaps right now isn't the time to tell her that.'

He kissed Neva on the lips and she hurried away before the ambulance came to a halt.

Back inside the house, Neva went to the library and phoned Jo.

'Mum and Dad and the rest of my family are on the way back to Surrey. It already feels odd knowing I'm here on my own.'

'Er. You're hardly on your own, are you? Apart from your adoring boyfriend, there's an entire houseful of people.'

'I meant, without my family. And speaking

of family, how's Charmaine?'

'Definitely not family. And never will be.' Jo sighed down the phone. 'I've made my final decision, Neva. I'm telling Rob this weekend, once his delightful family has left.'

'It's over?'

'Well and truly. Oddly enough, I do still love him in a way. But these last few days have made me realise it's not going to work. I shouldn't have said yes in the first place. I'm not doing that again in a hurry. The next time someone proposes and asks me to move in with them, I'm saying no.'

'Does he have any idea what's about to happen?'

'I think he might have an inkling. We haven't exactly been getting on over the holiday. New Year was a bit of a damp squib, as I told you and now we're hardly saying two words to one another. We go to bed and it's as much as we can do to wish one another a good night. He may not be as surprised or disappointed as you think.'

'I'm here if you need me,' Neva said. 'Good luck with it. Call me and tell me how it goes. I'm staying on here until Monday, but if you need me to come back to the flat before then, just give me a call, OK?'

'OK. I'm hoping Rob will move my stuff back to the flat in his van, but I'm not holding my breath on that, so this could be fun. Did you ever sort out a removal company for your stuff? Because if I'm now coming down to live with you, which I am, we'll need a bigger van.'

'I didn't. You know me. But luckily, Rafe and Adam know a man. I'd sort of assumed from our previous conversations that you'd be joining me, so Rafe's organised a van large enough to accommodate your stuff as well as mine. Oh, and did I mention, we're not going to be staying with Mum and Dad until the new place is mine? We're going to be staying at Wynter House.'

'We are? Wow. I'm definitely looking forward to that. Er. Does Olivia know?'

'Not yet. But she soon will. She's just arrived home in an ambulance, as we speak. Which is why I'm hiding in the library, calling you. It'll be lovely to have you here. And Adam says he's looking forward to meeting you.'

'Ditto. I really need to have some fun after this miserable Christmas and New Year.'

'Promise me one thing, Jo.' Neva was serious now. 'Adam's gorgeous and he's a lovely guy, but as I said before, I don't think he's really your type. Don't rush into anything just to get over Rob, will you?'

'You also said Rafe wasn't *your* type. And look at the pair of you now. But don't worry. I'll be careful. I'm certainly not looking for another relationship just yet. And from what you've told me about Adam, nor is he. What's the harm in both of us having a bit of fun?'

'None. I just don't want to see anyone get hurt, that's all.'

'We're both adults, Neva. And it takes two to tango. If we do fancy one another, I'll make it perfectly clear that fun is all I'm looking for. If he's not on board with that, I promise I'll keep my distance.'

'Thanks. I hope Adam feels the same.'

'We'll soon find out. Oh. I think the Ashfords are finally leaving. I'd better go and say goodbye. And then I'm really going to celebrate. Until tomorrow, when I'll break the news to Rob. If you don't hear from me again, you'll know he didn't take it well.'

'Don't joke about things like that, Jo. The last thing I need is to find you buried in Rob's new garden.'

'I've always said that Upminster is the end of the line. Speak to you tomorrow. Love you.'

Neva knew Rob wasn't a violent man, but even so, as she wished Jo good luck and said goodbye, she couldn't help but feel a tiny twinge of anxiety. Rob Ashford was already history as far as Jo was concerned, but after four years of dating and Rob's proposal of marriage, Rob may not take it as well as Jo was clearly hoping he would.

But then again, perhaps he might. People were full of surprises.

Chapter Eleven

Hazel Smart had only been at Wynter House for two hours and she was already beginning to wish she had taken another assignment. She had been told that Olivia Wynter would be a difficult patient but that hadn't worried her at all. She had dealt with difficult patients before and once she had gained their trust, the patients had all mellowed. She prided herself in the knowledge that she could turn the most cantankerous person into an amiable being within a matter of hours, or at worst, a day.

On meeting Olivia, she realised she was going to have her work cut out. The woman wasn't just difficult; she was obnoxious, snooty and intentionally cruel.

The first words out of Olivia's mouth had been aimed at making Hazel feel small.

'How do I know you're qualified to take care of me? You look like one of those dreadful, so-called glamour models rather than a nurse. The sort of woman who reveals her breasts for money. Those must have cost a fortune.'

'Thank you, Mrs Wynter. But they're real. As for my qualifications, I have a doctorate in nursing practice. A DNP is the highest level of qualification for a nurse. It means I can actually make diagnoses in certain circumstances.'

'Hmm. Not good enough to be a doctor.'

'I chose not to be. My mother was a nurse, and so was my grandmother. I wanted to follow in their footsteps. Patient care is what interests me.'

'Of course you would say that. I don't need a nurse. I have staff. They can take care of me.'

'I'm afraid they can't. And it was your grandson who decided that you needed a nurse. I'm sure once we get to know one another we'll get along nicely.'

'Get to know one another? You're an employee. I have no desire to "get to know" you, or vice versa. If I must have you with me, I hope you'll know your place. Do your job and stay out of my way as much as possible. Then, and only then, will this ludicrous situation work.'

After their initial meeting, Olivia hadn't said a word. She had closed her eyes and pretended to be asleep. Hazel could tell she was faking but the silence suited her. Even when Olivia was transported to the ambulance that would take her home, she only briefly opened one eye, quickly closing it again when she saw

Hazel was watching her. It was only when they reached the impressive drive to Wynter House that Olivia opened her eyes fully and as they pulled up at the porticoed front door, she spoke again.

'This ambulance driver should be sacked. I felt every bump in the road but at least I'm home at last. Once we're inside and I'm in my rooms, I want a cup of tea. I'm parched.'

'I'll see what I can do.'

'That's not an auspicious start.'

The ambulance doors were opened and two paramedics, one of whom had been sitting in the front with the driver, moved Olivia into a wheelchair and onto the tail gate lift.

'Ah, Rafe. Thank heavens.' Olivia suddenly looked frail. 'Where's Carruthers? Get me out of this bone shaker and up to my rooms. I'm completely worn out. If this nurse is the best the agency can do, I'm astonished they're still in business. It's so good to be home. That hospital has gone downhill since I was last there.'

'Welcome home.' A rather handsome man, around Hazel's own age, smiled at Olivia before turning his attention to Hazel. 'Hello. I'm Rafe Wynter and this is my brother, Adam. You must be Hazel Smart. Welcome to Wynter House. Is it OK for us to call you Hazel, or would you prefer a more formal address?'

Hazel smiled in return. Adam was just as

handsome as his clearly, elder brother. Not that she was interested in what they looked like. She was here to do a job. Not get involved with a member of the family. A friend of hers had been foolish enough to do that at her last assignment and it hadn't ended well. Hazel was determined she was never going to make that mistake.

'Hazel is fine. It's nice to meet you both.'

The tingle she got when Adam shook her hand wasn't quite so nice, or the ripple of electricity that she felt when he beamed at her.

'It's lovely to meet you, Hazel. I almost wish I still had that awful Norovirus. I wouldn't mind you taking care of me.'

Olivia tutted loudly. 'Adam. The woman is my nurse, not your latest plaything. Where *is* Carruthers?'

'I'm here, ma'am.'

'You're no use there. Come here and take me to my rooms. Judith? Ah, there you are. Show this woman where she's staying. I hope you haven't put her anywhere near me.'

A timid-looking but attractive woman, also probably in her mid to late thirties, stepped forward. She was obviously Judith, and she shot a look at Rafe. He was the one who answered.

'Hazel's room is next to yours, Olivia. Please don't cause a fuss. She needs to be close by in case of an emergency. It's either that, or you'll have to return to the hospital. None of us has time to take care of you, day and night. And Hazel comes highly recommended. Let's give this a chance, shall we? For all our sakes.'

'Do I have a choice?'

'No.'

'Something's got into you lately, Rafe, and I really don't like it. I don't like it at all.'

'I'm in love, Olivia. Surely even you remember how that feels?'

Olivia glowered at him but snapped at the man dressed as a butler. 'Carruthers? Why are we still here? I'll catch pneumonia next.'

'I apologise, ma'am.'

'Let me do that,' Adam said, taking the butler's place.

'We'll let you settle in, Hazel,' Rafe said. 'Judith will show you your room and if you need anything, just ask. Join us for lunch in the dining room at 1 p.m. and we'll introduce you to everyone else. We currently have several guests and there is a small staff.'

'Thank you. I'll see you at lunchtime.'

Adam gave the wheelchair a shove on the drive and it trundled to the front door.

Hazel took the opportunity to have a good look at the house. The size of it had struck her as they had approached along the drive. She hadn't expected it to be so large. She definitely hadn't thought it would be quite so beautiful. There was something rather welcoming about the façade.

The house was built of red stone and consisted of a central portion with large, mullioned windows, either side of which were protruding towers. Each tall, square tower bore onion-shaped, lead roofs which glistened in the light. To the left and right of those, were two identical blocks, each larger than the central portion, again with mullioned windows. Sunlight would stream into the house from every angle.

There were holly and a variety of other bushes, across the frontage of the house and rows of fairy lights were entwined in each and also around the portico. It must look magical at night.

To the left of the house, in the near-distance was a large barn, and another structure almost out of view, although the most distant one looked like a rather impressive building in its own right, even if it was on a much smaller scale than the house.

'So Hazel,' Adam said, beaming at her once more. 'How is your first day going so far?'

'About the same as usual,' Hazel lied, walking beside Adam and her patient.

This day was nothing like any she had experienced before.

She would have to be very careful at Wynter House. She had already felt a completely unexpected attraction to Adam Wynter, a man who was a bit of a womaniser, based on Olivia's comment.

But Olivia might not be telling the truth.

Rafe was in love with someone; someone of whom Olivia clearly disapproved. Judith was frightened of Olivia and possibly a little in love with Rafe, and perhaps with Adam too from the way she looked at them both. Carruthers wouldn't let anything ruffle his calm and no doubt competent demeanour.

And Wynter House was huge, with apparently more people for her to meet.

Yes. She definitely should've taken another assignment.

Chapter Twelve

'I've managed to get hold of Amelia,' Adam informed Rafe, as he sat down at the dining table for lunch.

Rafe furrowed his brows. 'Amelia?'

Neva sighed. 'The one with the fantastic body, according to Adam.'

'I don't recall saying fantastic.' Adam winked and grinned at her. 'I only said good. Like her name.'

'You said "very good", Adam,' Gavin reminded him.

Adam shrugged. 'You'll soon see for yourselves. She's agreed to come and stay for the weekend and for a few days into next week. She needs to be back in London by next Friday, but if things go well while she's here, she can come back and stay for longer. Possibly a week but maybe more, depending on what it is you and Sean want to achieve, Rafe, and whether she thinks she can be of help. Then she's off skiing for a fortnight.'

'Oh. The woman you said might be able to

help us with our marketing.' Rafe nodded. 'That sounds good. Have you told Judith? She'll need to have a room prepared.'

'Already done,' Judith said, walking towards them with an extremely buxom and attractive woman whom Neva hadn't yet met.

'Hello. You must be the nurse. I'm Neva. Lovely to meet you, Hazel.'

Hazel smiled. 'Hello, Neva. It's lovely to meet you too. Let me guess. You're Rafe's girlfriend?'

'How did you know that?'

'The fact that he was holding your hand when we walked in was a bit of a giveaway.'

Neva blushed, although she had no idea why, and Rafe merely smiled.

'Let me introduce you to everyone, Hazel.'

He gestured towards each person as he said their name and gave a brief statement concerning whether they were staff, or guests.

'It'll probably take you a while to remember us all,' Gavin said, but if you want anything fixing, lifted or carried, you can find me either somewhere around the grounds, or in my office, or my workshop at the rear of the house.'

Ethel smacked her gums together and chuckled loudly. 'The men will be lining up to be of service to you, young lady. Rafe's taken, as you can see, and Cecil and Ronnie aren't your type, but Adam and Gavin are young, free and single.'

'I don't have a type, but thank you for letting me know.' Hazel smiled at Ethel and at Gavin but seemed to be avoiding Adam's stare.

'Have you strangled Olivia yet?' Ethel added.

Hazel glanced at Neva and at Rafe. 'I'm here to take care of her.'

'Good luck with that,' Ronnie said.

'Tell us a little about yourself,' Adam coaxed, in a somewhat honeyed tone.

Without looking at him, Hazel reeled off her qualifications.

'Very impressive,' Queenie said, smiling. 'You must be in great demand.'

'Most nurses are. There's a shortage even in the private sector. I specialise in geriatric nursing but throughout my career I've cared for patients of all ages and with a variety of illnesses, long-term and life-limiting conditions, and disabilities.'

'It sounds as if you've got a wealth of experience,' Neva said. 'Olivia is clearly in very capable hands.'

'What about your personal life?' Adam asked.

Hazel blushed a little and darted a quick glance in his direction.

'I try to keep my work and my personal life completely separate. I'm here to work. I believe my CV provides all the relevant information.'

Ethel gave a burst of laughter. 'In other words, young Adam, mind your own business.'

Adam grinned. 'Yes, Ethel. I think I got the message, thank you. But it won't stop me from asking.'

'Excuse my brother,' Rafe said, throwing Adam a half amused, half reprimanding look. 'Sometimes he forgets that not everyone finds him irresistibly charming.'

Hazel smiled but she still didn't seem to want to look at Adam.

Neva studied her for a moment. Perhaps Rafe was wrong. Perhaps Hazel had already succumbed to Adam's undeniable charms. She had done so herself when she and Adam first met. It was only once she'd got to know Rafe that she realised it was Rafe she found irresistible, not Adam.

She must phone Jo after lunch and tell her that she may have some major competition as far as having fun with Adam was concerned. Especially on the boob front. Hazel's nursing skills weren't the only impressive things about her. And Adam probably wasn't that interested in her nursing capabilities.

Even this Amelia Goodbody might come in second.

A sudden thought popped into Neva's head. She would be leaving here herself on Monday and wouldn't be returning for another four days, meaning Rafe would be at Wynter

House with not just one exceedingly gorgeous woman, but two, if what Adam said about Amelia was true. And Neva didn't like that idea at all. It wasn't that she didn't trust Rafe. She did. But their relationship was new. And as she had discovered for herself, anything can happen at Wynter House.

Chapter Thirteen

Amelia pulled up outside Wynter House and smiled. The place was as beautiful as she remembered. Would Adam, and more importantly, his elder brother Rafe, be as gorgeous as they had been in the summer? At that time, they were both tanned, and after playing cricket in the sweltering heat, were just wearing shorts for the remainder of the day. Along with Gavin, their estate manager, they were enough to make a girl's hormones go haywire.

Amelia's hormones had definitely gone haywire when she'd seen Rafe. He made her own boyfriend seem pale and uninteresting. But then she'd always liked her men strong and moody-looking. Rafe and Adam's dark hair and incredibly blue eyes, only added to their charms. And the fact that Rafe had seemed so distant and unapproachable, made his appeal that much greater. She couldn't wait to renew the acquaintance.

She got out of her BMW Z3 and strode

towards the door which opened before she reached it.

'Ah. You're Carruthers, aren't you? My bags are in the boot. It's unlocked. Have you told Adam that I'm here?'

He made a slight bow. 'Mr Adam is with his grandmother at the moment, Miss Goodbody. He asked that you join him in the drawing room for drinks at 8 p.m. once you've freshened up. Miss Thorn will show you to your room.'

'Good evening, Miss Goodbody.' A woman who appeared just behind Carruthers smiled at her. 'I'm Judith Thorn. I don't suppose you remember me from your last visit.'

'No.' Amelia glanced at her watch. She could only just make out the time from the glow given off by the myriad fairy lights surrounding the portico and entwined in the various bushes beneath the ground floor windows. 'Why isn't there better outside lighting? Oh never mind. Do I have time to have a bath? The drive was hellish.'

'It's just before 7, so there's plenty of time,' Judith replied.

'Plenty of time? That's only an hour. Let's not dawdle.'

In the hall, Amelia shrugged off her coat as another young woman appeared from the library, if Amelia's memory served her correctly.

'Ah, Neva,' Judith said, beaming at the woman. 'This is Amelia Goodbody.'

'So I see,' the woman said, giving Amelia a rather impertinent once-over. 'I mean ... Hello. I'm Neva, as Judith has just said. Sorry. Er. May I call you Amelia?'

'No.' Amelia tossed her coat towards the woman, whose mouth dropped, along with Amelia's coat to the floor.

'I believe there has been a mistake,' Carruthers said, quickly putting Amelia's many cases down and picking up the coat. 'Miss Grey is a very special guest of Mr Rafe's.'

The woman blushed and thanked Carruthers profusely.

Amelia looked her up and down. 'Oh? I wasn't aware. Ah wait. Are you someone from the flooded village?'

'Um. Yes and no. I was staying at one of the cottages with my family for the holidays and Rafe invited us all to stay here.'

'I see. In that case, if you're Rafe's guest then yes, you may call me Amelia. One has to maintain decorum. I assumed you were staff.'

'I'm not. Although after everything that's happened, we all pitch in like one big, happy family.' Neva smiled. 'You'll be joining us for cocktails, no doubt. I'll see you then, Amelia.'

There was a certain intonation in Neva's voice as she said Amelia's name. The woman was clearly offended, but Amelia wouldn't trouble herself with that. Neva was unimportant. Although hadn't Carruthers said that she was "a very special guest"? What precisely had he meant by that?

As soon as she was ensconced in her rather splendid room and the butler had left, Amelia asked Judith about her.

'Who exactly is Neva? From the way the butler behaved, anyone would think she was a member of the family.'

'In a way, she is. Or will be one day. She's Rafe's, I mean, Mr Rafe's girlfriend. They're head over heels in love.'

'Girlfriend? In love? Since when? He was definitely unattached in early August.'

'Since she arrived here for Christmas.'

'Since Christmas?' A burst of laughter escaped Amelia's lips. 'And they're head over heels in love? I find that very hard to believe. Especially as it's Rafe. He made it clear that love was the last thing he was interested in.'

'But then he met Neva and it was love at first sight. But I probably shouldn't be telling you this. I'm sure he'll tell you himself. Is there anything else I can do for you, Miss Goodbody?'

'You can get me a glass of wine. A large glass. No. Champagne. And quickly. I want to drink it whilst I bathe.'

'I'll bring it myself, right away.'

Judith hurried to the door and Amelia took

off her Gucci suede pumps and tossed them across the room.

Rafe had a girlfriend. Damn the man.

There was always Adam. He was a very close second.

But Adam didn't own Wynter House. Rafe did.

And Amelia didn't like being in second place.

Something would have to be done about this Neva, woman. And the sooner the better.

Chapter Fourteen

Amelia sashayed into the drawing room and all heads turned in her direction. She was wearing a tight-fitting, black cocktail dress that must have cost a large fortune by the look of it and her make-up, hair and nails gave the impression that she'd got her own stylist stashed in her luggage.

She helped herself to a glass of champagne from several on a small table and made a beeline for Rafe, Neva, Adam and Sean.

'Adam! Rafe! It's wonderful to see you again. How kind of you both to invite me. I think you knew how taken I was with this house the last time I was here. And not just with the house.'

Neva didn't like the way Amelia was looking at Rafe. It was positively predatory. Like a panther eyeing up its prey, and she had crossed the room and was now standing so close to Rafe that she was almost in his pocket.

'It's good of you to come,' Rafe said, seemingly oblivious of Amelia's admiring glances.

'Adam thinks I may be able to help you with your new business, but he mentioned that funds are pretty tight.'

'They are.'

Amelia slipped her arm through his and tapped him playfully on the chest with her other hand.

'Let's not worry about that. I'm sure we can come to a mutually beneficial arrangement. I'm so excited to hear about this gin distillery of yours. Shall we find a cosy corner and put our heads together?'

Rafe looked surprised, but he wasn't as surprised as Neva.

Who did this woman think she was?

'Er. It's not just my distillery.' Rafe reached out and placed his hand on Sean's shoulder. 'Sean's my partner in this venture. And Adam, of course. But he's more of a sleeping partner. Have you met my girlfriend, Neva? I think we should wait to talk about business until tomorrow, if that's acceptable to you, Amelia? We'll be having dinner soon.'

With amazing dexterity, he extricated himself from Amelia's clutches. For a moment, she didn't look pleased but her mesmerising smile was soon back in place.

Which made Neva dislike the woman even more.

'Of course. And yes. Neva and I met briefly

when I arrived. I mistook her for staff.' She giggled coquettishly and gave Neva's dress a disparaging look as if it were nothing more than a rag. 'Sean, I believe we met at the cricket match. I never forget a handsome face. How are you?'

'I'd be better if my pub hadn't been flooded, but all in all, I'm good, thanks. How was the drive down?'

Amelia rolled her eyes and gasped. 'The roads were horrendous. But I had a luxurious bath and a glass of champagne shortly after I arrived and all seems right with the world once more. Well, almost.'

She gave Neva a dismissive glance.

Or was Neva imagining it?

'That's due to the weather,' Adam said. 'Months of rain followed by a flood. Then ice and snow and rain again isn't exactly ideal for these country roads.'

'I suppose that's the price one must pay to live in such a glorious house as this. I'd give anything to live here, you know. Absolutely anything.'

Amelia continued to ooze charm, like a snail trail, in Neva's opinion.

The good thing was, if this was how Amelia was going to behave, Neva needn't worry about leaving the woman with Rafe. He would never be taken in by such obviously false behaviour. And by throwing herself at him, Amelia would probably ensure Rafe would keep his distance.

Neva couldn't be more opposite to Amelia, and as he'd fallen in love with her, there was no way in the world he would be attracted to Amelia. At least, not in the long term. But the woman did have an unbelievably good body. There was no getting away from that. And legs so long they seemed to go on forever. She could look Rafe in the eye without the slightest tilt of her head. She must be over six feet in her heels.

Would Rafe be interested in a fling while Neva was away? Because Amelia couldn't have made it more apparent that she was offering just about anything. And from the sultry looks she was giving Rafe, that probably included sex.

'Hazel!'

Adam sounded surprised, and everyone's attention turned towards the doorway.

Rafe smiled. 'Do come and join us, Hazel. You've met everyone else but let me introduce Adam's friend, Amelia.'

'Not just Adam's friend, Rafe,' Amelia said in honeyed tones, completely ignoring Hazel.

Hazel smiled. 'I'm pleased to meet you. I'm Mrs Wynter's nurse.'

Amelia threw her a perfunctory smile but Adam's smile was genuine.

'You look lovely.'

Hazel blushed. 'Thank you, but I know that's not true. I wasn't expecting to be joining you all for drinks and dinner so I didn't bring anything suitable to wear.'

'You do look lovely,' Neva said.

Hazel was wearing a pair of plain black trousers and a loose-fitting, fluffy jumper. Unlike her nurse's uniform, which although it was not tight-fitting, still showed almost every curve, this jumper hid her assets. Even so, or possibly because of that, Neva did think Hazel looked lovely. And like Neva, Hazel was virtually make-up free with just a hint of lip gloss and a flick of mascara. Her long blonde hair was loosely tied into a ponytail and it was clear that she had no particular desire to impress with her looks.

'I agree,' Rafe added. 'What would you like to drink? There's champagne, to celebrate the fact that Olivia is home, and to welcome both you and Amelia to Wynter House. Or something else if you prefer.'

'I'm not really a champagne drinker.'

'I can recommend the gin,' Sean's wife, Wendy said, coming across the room to join them.

'I do like gin. But only a very small glass, please. Um. Do I detect there's something about the gin that you're not telling me?'

'What makes you think that?' Sean asked.

'From the way some of you smiled when Wendy suggested it.'

'You're very astute.' Adam gave her an

admiring glance.

'I like to think I'm observant. It pays to be in my profession. So what's with the gin then?'

'It's the first batch from our own distillery. Well, Rafe and Sean's really, but I helped a little. I'll get you a glass. Ice and tonic?'

'Yes please.'

'Should you drink at all on duty?' Amelia queried, with her trade-mark smile.

Hazel gave her a friendly one in return. 'Strictly speaking, I'm no longer on duty. Mrs Wynter's asleep but she may need me during the night and the nurse the agency has sent to sit with her while I'm off duty, isn't a specialist in cardiac care, due to the last-minute nature of the booking. I'd rather be safe than sorry, but one small glass won't impair my abilities.'

'Hmm. We used that very line in a drink-driving awareness ad once,' Amelia said.

'Hazel is off duty and she's not driving anywhere.' Neva was growing increasingly tired of Amelia's manner. The woman would get on well with Olivia. It was as if they were cut from the same cloth.

'I'm happy to pass on the drink if you'd rather,' Hazel said to Rafe.

'No. Olivia's fine. She looked so much better when Adam and I popped in to see her earlier this evening. You deserve some time off. You've spent the entire day with her.' He grinned. 'Anyone would need a drink after that.'

'She's definitely made a miraculous recovery since this morning,' Hazel said, grinning. 'And the echocardiogram and the other tests the doctors have carried out this week showed there was no damage to her heart, so I don't have any concerns. Nevertheless, it's best not to take things for granted. Jennifer, the nurse who's with her now is very good.'

'Just not as good as you,' Adam said, handing Hazel her drink.

'I simply have more experience, and one or two more qualifications, that's all. Jennifer is more than capable. I'd just like to be around in case. It's best to be prepared for any eventuality.'

'I'm sure she is,' Rafe said. 'What do you think of the gin?'

Hazel took a sip and after a moment or two she raised her brows.

'Wow. I think you've got a winner here. Is it for sale yet? My mum and dad would love a bottle.'

Rafe beamed at her. 'We're just about to begin production.'

'Which is why I'm here,' Amelia said. 'I've already got a few ideas.'

'I bet you have,' Neva said.

But she was pretty sure they had nothing to do with the gin.

Chapter Fifteen

'Jo? Is everything all right?'

It was a silly question. Jo wouldn't even call at 6 a.m. on a Saturday when she had to go to work, so definitely not when she was on holiday leave, unless something was wrong.

'No, it bloody well isn't. Rob's dumped me! Can you believe that?'

'Sorry what? Did you say Rob's dumped you? Not that you've dumped him?'

'Yep. We've been up for most of the night talking. And when I say talking, what I really mean is arguing. You should've heard the things he said. It started about five minutes after his family left and it ended a minute ago when he slammed the door and walked out.'

'He's walked out? But it's his house.'

'He hasn't walked out for good. He's just "going to get some fresh air", or so he says. But he also said that he hopes I won't be here when he gets back because breaking up with me "hasn't been easy for him". The bastard.'

'Wait. What? He's asked you to leave? For

good?'

'Yep. I haven't called you in the middle of something, have I? Were you asleep? I'm sorry, Neva but I had to talk to you.'

'Don't worry about that. I was awake anyway. Rafe got up about fifteen minutes ago because he wants to make an early start in the distillery before Amelia bloody Goodbody starts pawing him. Those are my words, of course. Not his. But that's not important right now. Tell me exactly what happened.'

'I'm not entirely sure. We waved his family off and I said I needed a drink. A very large one. And he said, "There you go again. All you've done since the second my family arrived is moan about them and make bitchy remarks." Well I can tell you, I was stunned. There was I, building up to find a way to break it to him gently that perhaps we'd made a mistake by getting engaged and moving in together and instead, he lays into me with a cricket bat.'

'He hit you! Oh my God.'

'What? No! Of course he didn't. I meant it figuratively, not literally, you nutter. As if he would do that. The man's never laid a hand on me like that. But he was really angry and I've never seen him in such a temper. It was virtually non-stop. He accused me of being rude and unpleasant. Of treating his mum and his siter like dirt. Of ignoring him and his feelings. Of being lazy. Me! Lazy! Bloody cheek.

He was the one who wouldn't get off his arse to get himself a beer, and he calls me lazy. He said that every time he turned around I was on the phone to you. That I kept disappearing to the shed when I should've been entertaining his family and being a good hostess. A hostess! He made it sound like we were living in the fifties and that I should've been the perfect 'little woman' running around after him and his family and fulfilling their every whim.'

'It's as if he doesn't know you at all.'

Neva couldn't help but smile, although she was thankful Jo couldn't see it.

'And then he said that you're a bad influence on me and that he was hoping that once he got me away from you, I might change, but he was disappointed to discover I hadn't. Er. If he didn't like me as I was, why the hell did he go out with me for four years and then ask me to marry him and move in with him?'

'Did you ask him that?'

'Of course I did. Wait until you hear this. He said he liked lots of things about me and that relationships were all about compromise. I'll give him bloody compromise. Oh, and that neither of us was getting any younger and that he wanted a family before he reached forty. That was something he failed to mention. But this is the best bit. He said he fell in love with me, "despite my faults". Despite my faults! I'll tell you something, Neva. If there had been a cricket bat handy, I might well have hit him with it. Several times. "Despite my faults". I'll give him faults. I've a good mind to go and cut up his favourite shirt. But I'm not a vindictive woman.'

'What a complete jerk. Did he say what he thought they were? Your faults, I mean.'

'Oh yes. He reeled off a list as long as my arm. It was even longer than the list I'd made over the last few days about him. I did one of those pros and cons lists. You know. Just to be sure that breaking up with him was the right thing to do. But the things I didn't like about him weren't anywhere near as many as the things he didn't like about me. It just goes to show, doesn't it? You think you know someone and something like this happens. You believe a person is in love with you and all the time they're making a list – and no doubt checking it twice, given that he made it during the damn festive season – of the reasons why they're going to dump you.'

'I must admit, I'm surprised. I thought he was crazy about you.'

'Not half as surprised as I was, believe me. So that's that then. I'm no longer engaged. He even asked for the ring back. The bloody cheapskate. I threw it at him. It was childish, I know, but I couldn't help myself. He gave me a list – yep, another list. He's been a busy boy – of what's mine and what's his. I told him he could add the bloody awful jumper Charmaine gave me for Christmas to his list, because there was no way I would ever be wearing the crappy thing again. Which made him even angrier and he told me to leave right away. He said he had hoped that we could have an amicable break up but it was obvious we couldn't.'

'Not after him ranting about you having faults, you couldn't. Is he mad?'

'I know. I wasn't going to do that when I dumped him. I was going to say I'd realised I wasn't ready for marriage and moving in together and all that stuff. God. I wish I'd dumped him first. Mind you, he still would've told me exactly what he thought, and either way, I'd have got the lists. So anyway, I had to call you to get it off my chest. I'm fuming, as you can tell. And now I've got to get someone to move my stuff asap, and go back to an empty flat. Until you get back to London, that is.'

'There's no way I'm leaving you on your own at a time like this. I'll come back today. Or ... why don't you come here? I'll need to check with Rafe but I'm sure he won't mind. We'll be coming here once our sale completes, anyway, so a few days beforehand won't make much difference, I'm sure. I'll get up now and go and find him and I'll call you right back. In the meantime, can you see if you can get someone to move your stuff back to our flat? The removal people are booked. I meant to call and tell you that when Rafe told me, but things happened here and I forgot. Or perhaps you could talk to Rob, once he's calmed down and ask if you can leave your stuff at his place until then. I'm sure the removal men could make a detour via Upminster. And I could come with you, just in case.'

'In case of what?'

'In case Rob makes another list and you end up having more rows. Anyway, what do you think?'

'I think that's the best thing I've heard since last night when his bloody family said goodbye. And you're right. Rob probably will let me leave my stuff here till Thursday, once he's calmed down. Until today, he always seemed to be quite a reasonable guy. Call me back once you've spoken to Rafe. I can chuck some of my stuff in my car and be down by lunchtime at the latest. I love you, Neva Grey. And I'm so glad you're my friend.'

'Ditto. I'll call you in a few minutes.'

Chapter Sixteen

Not only did Rafe agree that Jo could come to stay, Rob calmed down enough to allow Jo to leave her things at his house until the end of the week. Although he did say she had better make sure she only took the things on the list and nothing belonging to him. And that she should leave the keys, even though he intended to change the locks.

'I was so tempted to tell him that there was nothing of his I would ever want to take,' Jo told Neva as they hugged outside Wynter House a couple of hours later. 'But I decided I was on dangerous enough ground as it was and merely smiled and thanked him. Change the locks, indeed. As if I'd want to go back there. Moving to Upminster was the biggest mistake of my life.'

'You're here now and that's all that matters. It seems like forever since I last saw you.'

Neva meant it. It was as if they'd been apart for years, not just for a little over two weeks, even though they had spoken on the phone almost every day.

'I know. I feel the same. I was so excited on the way here, I almost missed the turn-off and had to drive over the verge. I hope there weren't any traffic cameras or I'll be getting a fine and points on my licence.'

Neva laughed. 'I did the same when I came here. Well, not here. To the village. Someone should make the sign bigger and more visible. I'm so glad you're here. Oh. This is Carruthers. Carruthers, this is my best friend in the world, Jo Duncan. But before we go any further, please call her Jo. Not Miss Duncan.'

Carruthers raised one eyebrow whilst lowering the other and gave a slight bow.

'As you wish. May I take your luggage?'

Jo beamed at him. 'Lovely to meet you, Carruthers. You're exactly how I imagined you would be. We'll give you a hand. It's not just my luggage in there. It's some of my worldly goods. My ex-fiancé has just thrown me out.'

'My sympathies, Miss ... Jo.'

'Miss Jo?' Jo repeated, grinning, as Carruthers marched to the boot.

Neva grinned too. 'Don't worry. You'll get used to that. Carruthers struggles with informality.'

'Need a hand?' Rafe appeared from the side of the house and covered the distance between them in seconds. 'I was in the old barn and I saw you arrive. I'm Rafe. It's so good to finally meet you, Jo. Welcome to Wynter House.'

Jo smiled at him and winked at Neva as she ignored Rafe's outstretched hand and gave him a hug. Rafe looked a bit surprised but he gave her a somewhat awkward hug in return.

'Same here,' Jo said, releasing him. 'Thank you for letting me come and stay. This house looks magnificent.'

'Thank you. We're rather partial to the place. You're welcome here anytime.'

Jo grinned. 'You may regret saying that. Although Sasha's been staying here, hasn't she? I'm not as much trouble as her. I promise.'

He gave a quick laugh. 'We've grown rather partial to Sasha, too, as it happens.'

'Yeah. She's a great kid. Just a little weird. I assume Neva's told you my sorry tale.'

'Most of it, I believe. I hope you're not too upset.'

'I'll live, thanks. And after a day with my best friend, and possibly a glass or two of this gin I've heard so much about, later on, I'll be fine.'

'Consider it poured. Do go inside. It's freezing out here today. Archie and I will bring in your belongings.'

He kissed Neva on the cheek as he walked to the boot.

'Definitely a keeper,' Jo whispered. 'I like

him.'

She and Neva linked arms and ambled towards the door, each with one of Jo's bags from the back seat of her car, tucked under their other arms.

'I'm glad. I like him too.' Neva grinned at her.

Jo glanced over her shoulder. 'What's not to like? He's even more handsome in the flesh. Is Adam anything like Rafe? You said they were very similar in looks.'

'Adam looks just like him, from a distance, but close up, you can see the differences. And Rafe's more reserved than Adam. Until you get to know him. But you may have some competition on the Adam front. I thought he'd be flirting with Amelia but he seems to be spending a lot of time with Olivia since she came home yesterday and I think that may have something to do with Olivia's nurse, Hazel. Amelia's a bit of a cow, in my opinion. But Hazel's lovely. You'll like her.'

'Hold on a minute. Who *is* that?' Jo glanced to her right just as they reached the portico.

Neva peered around her friend. 'That's Gavin. He lives here. He's the estate manager but he's also the gardener and handyman. He's a bit of a Jack of all trades. But then so is everyone else who lives and works at Wynter House, it seems.'

Gavin was pushing a wheelbarrow towards the kitchen garden and either he hadn't spotted them, or he was pretending not to. But he wasn't the type of man to do the latter, so he was probably just too busy to notice. Perhaps he had his earbuds in and was listening to either the classical music he had told Neva he liked, or BBC Radio 4, which was his favourite radio station, so he'd said.

'Does he indeed? You failed to mention him. I'm definitely going to like it here.'

'I'm sure I told you about him. I'll introduce you later. He'll be at lunch, I expect. Which is in about an hour, so we'd better get you to your room and settled in.'

'I can't wait to see it. Wow. This hall is really something. Is the entire house like this?'

'Pretty much. The only modern things about it are the en suites, and they're nowhere near brand new. It's gorgeous, isn't it? But it takes a lot of looking after. Dad and Nigel gave Rafe a hand over the holidays by doing a few things here and there, and Rafe, Adam and Gavin are always fixing something, but Dad said the place is a labour of love. It needs constant attention. And money for its upkeep. Which is why it's so important that Rafe's gin is a success. The house reopens to visitors at the end of January but the income from that isn't enough to keep the place running.'

Jo grinned at her. 'You sound like the

mistress of the house already.'

Neva shook her head. 'I wish. But then again, I don't. I'm not sure that's a role I'd be particularly good at. And Olivia, I'm sure, will do everything she can to ensure that doesn't happen. A hairdresser at the helm of Wynter House. It's enough to make all the long-dead Wynters turn in their graves.'

'If you marry Rafe, she won't be able to do anything about it.'

'We've only been together since Christmas Eve, Jo, and as much as I like the idea, I know it's a bit too soon to be thinking about that. Even if I am. But I'm trying not to. Although Rafe and I did discuss it briefly last night. I'll tell you about that later. I keep telling myself to concentrate on my new business for now.'

Rafe and Carruthers caught up with them.

'We'll take these up,' Rafe said, 'and get out of your way. I'm sure you two have a lot to talk about.' He smiled over his shoulder as he and Carruthers walked up the stairs.

Neva and Jo smiled back.

'Thank you,' Neva said. 'We have.'

'Oh. I've got more news.' Jo returned her attention to Neva. 'I was due to go back to work next Saturday, after taking three weeks off. Most of it, unpaid leave, I might add. But I phoned the salon this morning and gave them notice. I emailed it over before I left the house. They said not to bother to go back. I thought they might ask me to work my notice period. I'm so relieved they didn't.'

'Do you think that's because the owner is a client and friend of Rob's?'

Jo shrugged. 'Possibly. But as I'd only started there in November, I only had to give one week.'

'That's good. It means you can start off this year as you mean to go on. New home, new job, and possibly, in the not too distant future, a new man.'

'I'll take the home and the job. The new man I can do without. I told you, I just want a fling. There's no way I'm getting involved with anyone for a while. But I can't go more than a few weeks without sex. A couple of months is the absolute maximum. I know a man isn't strictly necessary, with everything that's available. But I prefer the real thing. Call me old fashioned.'

Neva laughed as they made their way along the hall and Jo gasped when Neva stopped at the open door to the room where Jo would be sleeping.

'Bloody hell! This is like staying in a posh hotel.'

'Except we don't charge,' Rafe said, standing aside to let them in. 'I'm glad you like it.'

'Like it? I love it. Neva has been telling me how gorgeous the place is but I still wasn't prepared for this. And a four-poster bed! I've always wanted to sleep in one.'

Carruthers gave a small bow and left the room. Rafe smiled and stood beside Neva as Jo dashed across the room, kicked off her shoes and carefully lay down on the antique covers.

'I hope you've got everything you need, but please let Judith know if there's anything you require. Or Neva, of course, and she can tell either Judith or Carruthers.'

'Thanks. I think I might just stay here for the rest of the day.'

'Make yourself at home,' Rafe said. 'If you'll excuse me, I must get back to the distillery. Get Neva to bring you over if you'd like a look around.'

Jo sat upright, propping herself up with her arms outstretched behind her.

'It's not a secret now then? I don't have to peer through a hole in the side to see what's going on?'

Rafe glanced at Neva and grinned. 'Not since Christmas Eve, no. But if you want to do that, please feel free.' He kissed Neva on the lips and gave Jo a wave. 'See you both at lunch.'

He was gone before Jo had time to wave back.

Chapter Seventeen

'You're the famous Jo,' Adam said, giving her one of his devilish smiles as they met in the hall just before lunch.

At least he hoped it was a devilish smile and that it didn't look as if he had indigestion or something. Perhaps he shouldn't have nipped into the kitchen and tasted the mixture for the carrot cake Penny was making for afternoon tea.

Jo wasn't exactly what he'd expected but she was pretty, had curves in all the right places, and a look about her that shouted fun. Or perhaps that was just wishful thinking. He could definitely use some fun right now. Christmas had been chaotic, although he'd enjoyed it more this year than the usual, quiet Christmases they spent at Wynter House. Until Boxing Day, that is.

He'd thought the village flood, and everyone moving to Wynter House had been a massive upheaval. Discovering he and Rafe had a sister and a niece had exceeded that by far and the truth was, he wasn't handling the news as well as he'd hoped he would.

Rafe seemed to be coping with it far better. But then Rafe could cope with anything. He always had. That was one of the reasons Adam admired his brother so much. No matter what life threw at him, Rafe would take it in his stride. Even heartbreak. He may bend, but he wouldn't bow or buckle. Rafe was strong, determined and had a sense of duty and responsibility that Adam couldn't hope to emulate. Even if he wanted to. Which frankly, he didn't.

Rafe took after their mother and grandmother in many ways. Adam leaned more towards their father. He wasn't weak. At least he didn't think he was. But change and upheaval bothered him in a way it never seemed to affect Rafe. And yet commitment bothered him far more. Especially where women were concerned. The thought of spending his life with one woman to the exclusion of all others brought him out in hives. Marriage wasn't something that appealed to him. At least that meant that, unlike his father, he would never break any marriage vows.

Anyone who met Adam and Rafe always thought that Adam was the fun-loving, cheerful and optimistic brother and Rafe was serious, moody and downright miserable at times. But nothing could be further from the truth.

Adam needed to have fun. He got so easily bored. He was rarely content with life or anything it offered. When he was in London, he longed to be at Wynter House, yet when he was here, he longed for the nightlife of London.

For most of his life he had put on a cheerful exterior to hide the fact that he felt he never quite shaped up to Rafe in Olivia's eyes. He wanted people to like him and say good things about him. He always hoped the future would be better than the past, but he never really did anything to make it so.

Rafe, on the other hand, found joy in the simple pleasures of life. A walk around their land, a swim in the pool beneath the Falls, the sound of birdsong in the spring, and even working on the house brought him happiness and contentment.

Rafe didn't care what anyone thought of him and never tried to be anything but himself. He took his responsibilities to the house, the Wynter name and those who depended on him, very seriously. But he had no time for pomp, or ceremony, or airs and graces, like Olivia. He treated everyone he met, the same.

Yes, he was prone to moods, but only because he strove to be the best he could be and was disappointed in himself when he failed. That was something he and Adam had in common.

Unlike Adam though, Rafe never really

knew how to flirt with women. If he liked someone, he found it hard to hide the fact. If he didn't, he found it equally difficult to hide his feelings. But when Rafe fell for someone, he fell deeply. When Adam fell for someone, it lasted for about three weeks.

Not that Adam had ever actually fallen in love. Only in infatuation. And he was infatuated with three different women right now. Four, if he counted Neva. But he didn't. Not now that she was with Rafe.

Amelia, Hazel and now Jo, though, were all young, free and single. And Adam desperately needed some fun. And some sex. At this moment in time, he didn't really have a preference of the three. They were all attractive, sexy and appealing in different ways. He could flirt with all three and see where that might lead. But one thing Adam wouldn't do, is date more than one woman at a time. And he drew the line at sleeping with more than one woman in the same week. Something his father had clearly had no qualms about.

There was a chance that none of them would be interested. If that was the case, he had really lost his touch. But Jo was smiling at him in a way he'd seen so many times before. Unless he was greatly mistaken, fun wasn't too far off.

'I don't know about famous,' Jo said, flicking her hair in a provocative manner. 'Infamous is probably more apt. I suppose you've heard about my broken engagement.'

'No. Well ... not in detail. Neva did mention that you felt you'd made a mistake and might be moving down to Merriment Bay in the very near future.'

Jo glanced at Neva. 'You haven't told him?'

'The only person I've told is Rafe. It's not my place to discuss your relationships, especially with people you haven't met.'

'If you need a shoulder to cry on,' Adam said. 'Both of mine are free.'

'Cry is the last thing I want to do. But thanks for the offer. Now if you've got a spare hand to lead me into temptation, or just to show me somewhere around here to let my hair down, so to speak, I'll take you up on that.'

'Jo!' Neva looked shocked. 'You've only just arrived.'

'Yes. But I've just been cooped up in a house with a bunch of people whose idea of a good time is wearing awful jumpers and playing scrabble. Would you begrudge your best friend in the world a bit of a giggle?'

'Of course I wouldn't. But I don't want to see you get hurt.'

'Your friend will be safe with me,' Adam said.

'Forgive me, Adam, but I'm not sure I'm convinced.' Neva smiled as she shook her head.

'I've just got out of a very long relationship,' Jo said. 'I'm not looking for another one. I'm a big girl, Neva. I can take care of myself.'

Neva shrugged. 'I know you can. I suppose I was hoping we could spend some time together.'

'I want that too. But perhaps I could also spend an hour or two with Adam? I'd love a tour of the house.'

Adam smiled. 'It's at its best during the evening. Why don't I take you on a guided tour after dinner tonight?'

'That sounds perfect to me.'

He held out his arm to lead Jo and Neva into lunch and he only just heard Neva's mumbled remark.

'That sounds like a euphemism for sex, to me.'

Which only made his smile wider as they entered the packed dining room and he clapped his hands together to get everyone's attention.

'This is Neva's best friend Jo. Rather than Neva or myself doing the introductions, why don't we all do as Rafe suggested when we got together after the flood, and each take it in turns to say who we are and what we do?'

Jo gave him an amused look. 'Seriously?' OK. Shall I start? I'm Jo, as Adam said, I'm Neva's best friend and like Neva, I'm a hairdresser. I was engaged but now I'm not and I'm moving down to Merriment Bay next week to join Neva in her new business and to be her flatmate.'

'Her flatmate?' Rafe echoed from behind them.

'Yes,' Neva said, turning to smile at him. 'I told you Jo's going to be moving into the flat above the salon.'

'Yes. But I thought ... Um. It doesn't matter. We'll discuss it later. Sorry, Jo. Please continue.'

He walked over and slid his arms around Neva, kissing her neck as he did so.

'That's it really,' Jo said. 'Who's next?'

Cecil leapt to his feet, as Adam led Jo to a seat and sat beside her, followed by Neva and Rafe.

Ronnie was the next to speak and then Queenie until everyone around the table had said a few words, apart from Adam, Neva and Rafe.

'You know who we are,' Rafe said, laughing. 'The only person missing is Gavin. He won't be joining us for lunch because there's something he wants to get finished. You'll meet him at drinks later though.'

'And Hazel. Olivia's nurse,' Adam said. 'She's having lunch with Olivia, poor girl.'

'Oh yes. And, of course, Olivia. She's our grandmother. But Neva's probably told you about her.'

'A little. Yes. I saw Gavin briefly when I

arrived. Neva told me who he was. But won't he be cold and hungry? It's freezing out there, as you said earlier.'

'He's used to it. Penny took him out a flask of soup.'

Penny nodded. 'I did. There's no need to worry about Gavin, Jo. He thinks frostbite is a cold snack covered in white chocolate.'

'He was the only one at the Boxing Day dip who didn't wear a wetsuit of some sort, just trunks,' Neva said.

'Really?' Jo laughed, but she gave Neva a rather odd look. 'You didn't mention that when you called to tell me about how mad everyone is in Merriment Bay.' She glanced around the table. 'Did most of you go in the water?'

'Not me,' Ethel said. 'I stayed here and so did Queenie. Too cold for our old bones. Although we did it every year when we were younger. And our dear husbands did too.'

'My dogs, Boris and Duchess aren't fans of the sea,' Queenie added. 'They prefer a dip in the river. But only in the summer. And certainly not when it's as wild as it's been this year.'

'We didn't either,' Cecil said. 'We watched, but we didn't go in. The sea is so polluted these days and Ronnie's had a fear of sharks ever since we watched *Jaws* on one of the movie channels years ago.'

'I have. You'll probably laugh, but when

the village flooded that was the first thing I thought about.'

'Sharks?' Jo queried. 'But sharks don't live in rivers.'

'Fears aren't rational, darling. That's what makes them so frightening. I even panic if I take a bath. Which is why we had a shower installed as soon as we moved into Ruby Cottage.'

'It isn't that far-fetched,' Cecil added. 'Crocodiles have been found in sewers.'

Queenie nodded. 'Mabel and Lionel found a poisonous spider under the toilet seat and a snake in the shower. But that was at their son's house in Australia. The neighbour had an alligator in their fishpond. Or was it a crocodile? I get confused.'

'Who are Mabel and Lionel?' Jo glanced at Neva, who shrugged.

'No idea.'

Adam smiled. 'They live in the village but they go to Australia each year for a few months. They won't be back until February.'

Neva gasped. 'So they don't know about the flood?'

Rafe nodded. 'They do. I have their son's email address. I emailed as soon as I thought the river might breach and asked for permission to enter their home and save what we could, if necessary. They leave a key with Ethel. I've sent them photos. They were going to return early, but I told them there was no point. With any luck, the cottage will have dried out by the time they do come home.'

'I'd like to be in Australia right now,' Queenie said, with a sigh. 'I'm fed up with the cold weather.'

'No you wouldn't,' Ethel said. 'You're terrified of spiders, you don't like snakes and the closest you'd ever want to be to either an alligator or a crocodile is to have them as a handbag or a pair of shoes.'

'Oh, I did have a wonderful alligator handbag years ago,' Queenie said.

'So did Cecil,' added Ronnie. 'But it's not the done thing these days.'

'We had a lion here once,' George, the retired estate manager and former gardener piped up. 'I was a boy at the time and my father brought me to see it. It was a wedding present to Olivia and your grandfather from one of her relatives in Kenya.'

'As a trophy, lion skin rug, you mean?' asked Jo.

'No. A living, breathing, roaring lion. You'd be surprised the things that came in and out of this country in those days.'

'Olivia never told us about it, did she Rafe?' Adam glanced at his brother.

'No. But of course it wasn't the only thing she didn't tell us. What happened to it, George?'

'Olivia wanted to keep it but your grandfather said it was cruel. They were going to give it to a zoo, but he didn't like that idea either. Ended up paying a lot of money to get it transported back to Kenya with a friend of his who was going out there to live. There was a photograph of it somewhere. But it was taken down along with all the others after your grandfather's death.'

'I'm going to ask Olivia about it,' Adam said.

'Tempest was a bit like a lion,' Queenie said.

Roger, Penny's husband tutted. 'More like a wolf.'

'A cuddly wolf,' Taryn, Sean's daughter said. 'I'd love to have a pet wolf.'

Ethel chuckled. 'I've had a few wolves in my time. But they were of the two-legged variety.'

Jo sniggered. 'Is it always like this?'

Adam grinned at her. 'The conversations, you mean? Yes. Since the flood and everyone coming to stay. Prior to that, conversations during lunch were usually about our dwindling finances, the numbers of paying guests, or what needed repairing next. Tell me, Jo. Would you like to pet a wolf?'

She grinned at him, cocking her head to one side. 'Is that a line, Adam Wynter? If so, it's a bad one. And completely unnecessary.' She leant closer to him and whispered in his ear. 'You had me at the dining room door.'

He nearly choked on the mouthful of wine he'd just swallowed.

Chapter Eighteen

Neva loved Jo as much as she loved her own sister but at that moment, she wasn't sure she liked the way Jo was behaving. They'd joked on the phone about Jo and Adam getting together, but Neva hadn't expected her best friend to throw herself at the man the minute they met.

What would Rafe make of such behaviour? And Olivia? The woman would probably have Jo tarred and feathered and banished from the county if she found out. Along with Neva, for inviting such a brazen hussy into the hallowed halls of Wynter House.

Or was Neva being overly dramatic?

She wouldn't usually find fault with Jo's behaviour. Jo had always been a bit of a free spirit. It was one of the many things Neva loved about her. Jo had always been a bit of a flirt as well. It had never worried Neva before. Why did it matter now? She was getting as bad as Rob. Friends didn't criticise one another. Especially best friends.

Jo had just been through a breakup and

was no doubt an emotional wreck, even though she was doing an excellent job of hiding the fact. Perhaps letting off some steam with Adam wasn't such a bad thing. Better than spending her days and nights crying, which is probably what Neva would have been doing right now if she were in Jo's shoes.

And they were both adults. It wasn't Neva's place to play some sort of chaperone to Jo, and she had no control whatsoever over Adam. If he wanted to have a fling with Jo and Jo wanted the same, who was Neva to get in the way of that?

But what she really didn't want was for either of them to get hurt. Or to hurt anyone else with their actions. Rafe had enough to contend with. Neva didn't want to add to his burdens. If things didn't go well between Jo and Adam, that was what might happen. And there had already been quite enough drama at Wynter House.

Perhaps a quiet word with Jo might help.

After lunch, Adam and Rafe went off to the distillery along with Amelia and Sean, which meant Neva and Jo could spend some time together. As usual, Neva had offered to help clear away the lunch things but Penny shook her head.

'We'll be fine, Neva. You and Jo can go and have a good old catch up.'

Neva smiled and turned to Jo.

'Let's go somewhere quiet and have a chat.'

'Why don't we go outside and get some fresh air?' Jo suggested.

'It's freezing out there.'

'A brisk walk in this country air will do us good.'

Jo linked her arm through Neva's and they walked out into the hall.

'Hmm. Are you sure this is about us getting some fresh air and not about you getting a closer look at Gavin?'

'I wouldn't mind getting a look at the local flora, fauna and other life on the Wynter estate. And you could do with some colour in your cheeks. You're looking a bit pasty. I think you've been spending too much time indoors. Although if Rafe, or Adam, was my boyfriend, I'd probably do the same.'

'I don't look pasty.' Neva glanced at her reflection in one of the elegant, antique mirrors hanging in the hall, dotted between various family portraits and other works of art. 'Do I?'

She had been spending quite a lot of time indoors since coming to Wynter House. Especially in the library. Perhaps she did look a little washed out. But she had been worrying about quite a few things lately. Like her new business and what she'd need to do to make it a success. She worried about the fact that Olivia didn't like her, despite making jokes about it. She worried about her sister being left alone to run the family business, miles away from their parents and from her. Rowan wasn't alone, of course; she had Nigel. And Sasha. But until now, Rowan had also had the benefit of having Dawn and Dennis just a few minutes away. How would she cope?

On top of that, Neva was also worried about moving out of Wynter House and leaving Rafe with Amelia. She trusted Rafe. She really did. But Amelia was gorgeous, exceedingly clever, tall and business-savvy. The woman knew what she wanted and how to get it. And it was clear to Neva that Amelia seemed to want Rafe. Could he be swayed by her abundant charms? Especially if Neva wasn't around.

'You do look tired,' Jo said. 'Come on. Let's get outside. Then you can explain why you were giving me such dour looks during lunch. And please don't say you weren't, because we both know you were.'

Neva sighed as they put on their coats and headed out onto the drive. It wasn't nearly as cold as it had been earlier and the afternoon sun was warm on Neva's face. She closed her eyes for a moment and tipped her head back to take full advantage of every golden ray.

'I'm sorry,' she said, opening her eyes after a few seconds and smiling at Jo. 'You're right about the looks. But you and Adam were flirting rather a lot during lunch.'

Jo grinned. 'We were. He's gorgeous and it

was fun. I haven't laughed so much in ages. He's really good company, isn't he? So why the looks? I told you what I was doing. Are you worried Rafe won't approve? Or possibly, Olivia? You want her to like you, don't you?'

Neva sighed again. 'Yes. But I know she never will. I'm not good enough in her eyes.'

'It's not her eyes that matter. It's Rafe's. And any idiot can see that his sparkle every time he looks at you. Even the way he says your name sounds like a caress.'

Neva beamed at her. 'I thought I imagined that. But you're saying you can hear it too?'

'Loud and clear. And unless Olivia is stone deaf, she'll also have heard it. She may not like you, but she's going to have to accept you. I don't think there's any doubt that you're here to stay as far as Rafe's concerned.'

'Assuming he can withstand Amelia's ample charms.'

'Of course he can. Besides, according to Ethel, Hazel, the nurse is the one with ample charms. I'm looking forward to meeting her and seeing what my competition for Adam's attention, looks like.'

'Please be careful, Jo. Adam's lovely and he really is a flirt but he's also Rafe's younger brother.'

Jo stopped walking and turned to face Neva. 'And? I can feel a lecture coming on.'

Neva nudged Jo onwards and they

continued along the path towards the kitchen garden, where the sun lit up the ancient red brick wall and warmed the timbers of a weather-beaten oak bench.

'Not a lecture. Just a word of warning.'

'Aren't they the same thing?'

Neva shook her head and sat down with Jo beside her.

'No. A lecture is longer. I'll make this short.' She grinned at Jo. 'Adam flirted with me when I first arrived. He's flirted with Amelia and with Hazel. I think he flirts with every woman he meets. You've just come out of a serious relationship. I can't help thinking it may not be such a good idea to rush into anything with Adam.'

'Are you saying you'd rather I didn't sleep with your boyfriend's brother?'

'I'd never tell you who to sleep with. You know that. All I'm saying is that it might not be a good idea to do so on the first night you arrive.'

'Will it make things awkward for you and Rafe if I do?'

Neva shrugged. 'I don't know. It shouldn't. But that's the thing. I've only known them myself for a couple of weeks. I have no idea how Rafe might take it. But I do know how Olivia will. And her having another heart attack is not something I'd like to be a party to, in any way, shape or form.'

'So you would rather I backed off? Even though I'm desperate to have some fun. And some sex, come to that.'

'I would simply rather you wait for a day or two and give yourself some time to settle in and to think about this rationally and see if you're still so keen after that. And if Adam is too.'

'But isn't the whole point of having a fling, not actually thinking rationally about it? That's what makes it fun. Spontaneity isn't usually your thing, I know, but weren't you spontaneous when you fell in love with Rafe?'

'Yes. But I did think about it for a few days though. I didn't jump into bed with him the minute we met.'

'Ah. But that might be because he didn't ask you to. And because you didn't have the opportunity. But you fancied Adam when you first met him, didn't you? You told me that on the phone. And if you'd had the chance, wouldn't even you have acted on it?'

Jo had a point.

'I'm very glad I didn't have the chance. If I had, I probably wouldn't be with Rafe right now. But I would probably still have fallen in love with him. And then I'd have bitterly regretted my hasty actions.'

'So you're saying that I shouldn't have sex with Adam in case there's someone better out there? You're forgetting one important thing, Neva. I'm not looking for a relationship. Just a bit of fun.'

'I wasn't looking for a relationship either. And look at me now. I'm head over heels in love and wondering what Amelia and her perfect body might be doing right this minute to try to get her claws into the man I love. Because she definitely wants to get her hands on Rafe. I'm pretty certain of that.'

'Yeah. I agree with you on that score. I saw the way she was looking at the two of you at lunch. Daggers were flying at you, that's for sure. But as I said just now. Rafe only has eyes for you.'

'I thought you only had eyes for Adam during lunch.'

'Which proves my point. I'm not besotted with Adam Wynter. There's no danger of me falling in love with him. Or with him falling in love with me. No one's going to get hurt. I know you're worried about me. And also about Adam and about Rafe. And Olivia, too. But why should me and Adam having sex, be a problem for anyone else? I'll tell him we have to keep it a secret if that helps. That might make it more fun, in fact. We could sneak into each other's rooms in the dead of night. And maybe once or twice during the daytime, too. Depending on how good he is in bed. I do think he'd be really good. You said Rafe is sensational. Perhaps it's in their blood. Would you begrudge your best friend in the world, some really good sex when she hasn't had any sex at all since the day we both left London?'

Jo pulled a sad face and whimpered like a lost puppy and Neva burst out laughing.

'No. Oh God. OK. Fine. But don't come running to me if your heart gets broken. Or if Rafe or Olivia throw you out of the house for leading Adam astray. And yes I know. Adam doesn't need leading astray. He can make his own way there and clearly wants to. I'm just worried that this could all go terribly wrong somehow, that's all.'

'Don't be. Nothing is going to go wrong. Scouts honour. Or do I mean, girl guides pinkie promise, or something?'

Neva gave Jo a playful nudge.

'As you were neither, and nor was I, I haven't a clue. But whatever you do, I think it might be a good idea to keep it quiet. Not secret, exactly. But perhaps don't flaunt it. At least that way Olivia may not find out.'

'What was that?'

Jo whirled round on the bench and looked to her left.

'It sounded like something heavy landing on concrete.'

Neva jumped up and shot a look in the same direction.

From what appeared to be a hole in the wall but was clearly a door into the kitchen garden from the main grounds, Gavin appeared, a wry smile on his face and a shovel in his hand.

'Er. That would be me, dropping my spade. Sorry, Neva.'

Neva swallowed hard and her cheeks burned as she stared at him.

'Did ... did you hear what we were saying?'

He let out a sigh and ran a hand across his forehead, shoving his tousled hair from his dirt-smeared face. He wasn't wearing a coat, only a plaid shirt, jeans and boots and was covered from head to toe in soil.

'I could lie and say I didn't hear a thing. Or I could tell the truth and say I heard almost every word. I was going to call out but I didn't know what to do for the best. I would've walked away but I was in the middle of a hole at least four feet down.'

'Oh dear God.'

Neva looked at Jo, who was, for once, keeping quiet, although her mouth was open and she was staring at Gavin and blushing so much she could blend in with the red brick wall.

'There's no need to worry. I'm no gossip. My lips are sealed.' He glanced at Jo and with a serious look in his eyes, said, 'It's none of my business, and we haven't actually met, but I know who you are and what's recently happened, and Neva's right. You shouldn't jump into bed with the first man who shows an interest. That's never a wise move, in my opinion. Now if you'll excuse me, I'd better go and get cleaned up. Olivia wants me to fix a lock on the door between her room and Hazel's, and we know what Rafe's going to say about that.' He turned away to go back through the doorway but stopped and glanced over his shoulder. 'Oh yeah. I forgot to mention. Hazel probably heard the first part of your conversation. She was just walking away from delivering Olivia's message when the pair of you arrived. I may have imagined it, but her pace seemed to slow when you mentioned Adam's name. I thought you should know that. Enjoy the rest of the afternoon, ladies.'

Neva gasped. Jo closed her eyes and shook her head.

'Hazel heard? My God, Jo. What did we say when we first sat down?'

Neva was astonished that Jo hadn't told Gavin that her sex life wasn't any of his business but she had sat in silence and merely stared at him. Just like she was staring at Neva now.

'Jo? Did you hear me?'

Jo nodded, slowly. She seemed to be miles away.

'Um. I think you said that Adam flirted with you and with Amelia and Hazel and you thought he flirted with every woman he meets. Oh, and that you'd rather I didn't sleep with your boyfriend's brother on the first night I arrive. But I can't recall exactly, so I may be wrong. Er. Was it my imagination, or did Gavin look like he was judging me? And not in a good way.'

'Does it matter? You don't usually care what people think.'

'No. You're right. Of course it doesn't. It doesn't matter one little bit. And he shouldn't have bloody well been eavesdropping anyway. He should've shouted out the minute he heard us talk about sex. Perhaps the man's a pervert.' She raised her voice at that bit, no doubt so that Gavin could hear, but he didn't come back and he didn't say another word from the other side of the wall. 'Bloody men. Sometimes I wonder why we bother with them at all.'

Chapter Nineteen

Adam strolled into the drawing room much later than his usual 8 p.m. but not because he'd been busy, or late getting showered and dressed from his jeans and trainers into smart trousers and a shirt and jumper. It was because he'd sat staring out of his window for some time after he'd got dressed.

He must be coming down with something and he hoped it wasn't a return of the damn Norovirus because that was an experience he'd rather not repeat so soon.

But there must be something wrong. He definitely didn't feel quite right. Perhaps he'd caught a cold? Or maybe the flu. There had been several people at the hospital, coughing and sneezing over the last few days.

He hadn't coughed or sneezed though. He simply felt ... off colour. He should be looking forward to tonight. And yet, he wasn't. Jo had made it abundantly clear that she was keen to have some fun and they both knew what that really meant. He'd even changed his sheets straight after lunch in readiness, in case he didn't have time after helping out in the distillery, and he didn't want to ask Judith. She had quite enough to do these days.

But the odd thing was, the more he'd thought about it this afternoon – and he'd thought about it a lot – the less sure he was that he wanted to go through with it.

It wasn't because of Jo. She was attractive, sexy and had made it clear there would be no strings attached. So it must be because he was unwell. What other explanation could there be?

Now, as he crossed the drawing room to where Jo and Neva were deep in conversation with Hazel, Jo looked stunning. And yet he still couldn't summon his usual enthusiasm.

'Good evening,' he said, his voice sounding dry, even to his ears. 'You're all looking lovely tonight.'

'Oh, please,' Hazel mumbled, but loud enough that he heard it.

She turned to face him, giving him a look as if she wouldn't wipe her feet on him. Which was a pity, because she looked even more stunning than Jo and Neva put together. And even that was odd, because of the three women, Hazel was wearing the plainest and least glamorous clothes. Like last night, she wore black trousers but tonight she wore a blouse which was buttoned to just below her neck and a cardigan that wouldn't look out of place on

Olivia. And yet, somehow, Hazel managed to look sexy and very appealing even though not a hint of cleavage could be seen and if she had so much as swiped lipstick on her lips, it wasn't noticeable.

'You do look lovely,' he repeated, feeling a little irked that she didn't believe him.

She made a disapproving face. 'You say that to all the girls.'

That was a phrase he'd heard many times, but never with such distaste.

'Only if they do.'

She didn't look convinced.

'Thanks,' Jo said. 'You look lovely too.'

He glanced at Jo and smiled wanly. 'Actually, I think I may be coming down with something. I'm not feeling that brilliant.'

'Let's forget about tonight then,' she said, a little too quickly.

But he was pleased in a way. He felt as if he'd been let off the hook.

He was definitely not well.

'Hazel? I know you're Olivia's private nurse, but any chance you could give me a quick once-over? I'm definitely not feeling myself.'

Hazel gasped and shot a look at Neva and Jo before giving him a sarcastic smile.

'Surely you can come up with a better line than that, Mr Wynter? There's no way I'm going to be "feeling" you, if that's what you think. Excuse me, please.'

Adam darted a look from Neva to Jo and to Hazel's retreating back. She had made her remark sound light-hearted and yet he felt as if she had slapped his face.

'What did she mean by that? I thought nurses were meant to care for the sick.'

Neva and Jo exchanged glances but didn't say a word.

'What? Am I missing something? Hold on. I need a glass of water. My throat feels very dry. I really don't feel good.'

He poured himself some water from a large jug on one of the tables and gulped it down in seconds.

'You're serious?' Neva sounded surprised.

'Yes. I haven't felt right for the last hour or two.'

'We thought...' Neva's voice trailed off.

'What?'

Jo sighed. 'We thought it was a chat up line.'

'A chat up line?' He glanced over his shoulder but Hazel was nowhere in sight. 'Is that what Hazel thought? Is that why she walked off?'

Jo nodded. 'It's my fault. I was telling Neva this afternoon that I thought you were lovely but that I also thought you would flirt with any woman, just for fun. I think Hazel overheard.'

Neva blushed. 'Actually, Adam, it was me

who said that. Not Jo. She's trying to take the blame for me. I can't recall exactly what I said though. I'm sorry.'

He couldn't take this in. His head was swimming. He felt hot yet shivery. And he was starting to feel a little sick.

'It's true. I do flirt with most women. But why would that upset anyone?'

'Some women don't like men who flirt,' Jo said. 'Just like some men don't like women who do that.'

'Adam?' Rafe tapped him on the arm. 'Are you OK? You don't look your usual self.'

'That's exactly what I've been saying. I think I may need to go and lie down.' He glanced at Jo. 'That wasn't a chat up line.'

'I didn't think it was.'

She smiled but looked somewhat confused. Which was how he was feeling. Confused, light-headed and dizzy.

'Yes. I definitely do. I'll see you tomorrow.'

'Hold on,' Rafe said. 'I'll come with you.'

'You're not my type,' Adam quipped. 'And you're my brother.'

'And I'm worried about you. You were distracted earlier when I was telling you about an idea of Amelia's. I thought it was because you had your mind on ... on other things. But you're sweating, Adam. And shivering. Where's Hazel? I'm going to ask her to take a look at you.'

'Done that. She told me to get lost. In a roundabout way.'

'What? She's a nurse. Why would she do that? Oh. Did she think you were trying to chat her up? Never mind. Archie?' Carruthers appeared from nowhere, as if he knew his assistance would be required. 'Would you please go and find Hazel and ask her to come to Adam's room?'

'I can do that,' Neva said, the concern in her voice apparent. 'We all thought he was joking.' She dashed past them towards the door.

'Go with her, please, Archie. She doesn't know where Adam's room is. Neither of them will. Sean? Could you give me a hand? He's becoming a dead weight.'

Adam tried to focus on his brother. 'That's not a nice thing to say about me.'

'I'll say nice things when you're feeling better. Adam? Adam?'

Was he in a tunnel? Or had he fallen through a hole in the floor? Whatever it was, it was dark and cold, and clammy.

Chapter Twenty

'Sepsis!' Rafe's voice was hoarse. 'That can kill.'

'Which is why I've called an ambulance.' Hazel sounded a little croaky too as she stood beside Adam's bed.

'An ambulance?' Neva repeated, in disbelief and panic as she shot a look at Rafe. He looked dumbstruck.

Hazel had seemed concerned when Neva explained what happened after she had left the drawing room, and just seconds after she and Neva and Carruthers entered Adam's room, she had asked Rafe to help her remove Adam's jumper. Having taken his temperature and unbuttoned his shirt to listen to his heart and his breathing, she had pulled her phone from her trouser pocket and asked for an ambulance immediately.

'I'd rather you hadn't heard me tell the emergency services that,' she said, as she undid the remainder of his buttons. 'I'm not saying it is. The symptoms of sepsis are very similar to the flu, which is why sepsis is often overlooked.'

'The flu can be serious too,' Neva said, taking Rafe's hand in hers.

She felt sick with fear. Rafe would be feeling terrified. He was watching Hazel in silence as she appeared to be looking for something on Adam's torso and arms. She stopped suddenly and grabbed her bag containing a range of her medical equipment, pills and bandages.

'It can,' Hazel said. 'But not usually for someone of Adam's age. If it is sepsis, it's in the very early stage, I believe, but I don't have the antibiotics required to treat it. If the paramedics know there's a chance it could be sepsis, they'll know it needs to be diagnosed and treated without delay. The best way to treat it though, is to get him to A&E. Please try not to panic.'

She took a packet from her bag and wiped something on Adam's arm. Then she removed a plastic cap from what looked like a needle.

Neva turned her head away. She didn't like injections and didn't want to see whatever it was that Hazel was doing. But a few seconds later she turned her head back and saw that Hazel had attached what looked like a thin tube and a clear bag of liquid to Adam's arm via that needle, over which Hazel had placed a piece of surgical tape. Hazel then hung the bag on a sort of fold away stand she had set up on Adam's bedside table. Having done that, she turned and gave Rafe a reassuring smile.

'It could be a number of things,' she said. 'What concerns me is the fact he passed out. But that could be due to dehydration, which is why I'm giving him fluids. The recent Norovirus Neva said you've all had has caused that. When the ambulance arrives, I'll go with them. You'll no doubt want to join us at the hospital. The night duty nurse with Mrs Wynter can handle anything until I return. Will someone let the paramedics in as soon as they arrive?'

'I'll do that,' Sean said. He'd been standing in the doorway looking as worried as the rest of them.

'Anything I can do?' Jo asked from the doorway as Hazel returned her attention back to Adam.

'Stay with Neva, please,' Rafe said, finally speaking after he let out a long breath as if he'd been holding it in for quite a while. He looked Neva in the eye. 'I can't believe we're going through this again so soon after Olivia's heart attack. I'll call you as soon as I know anything. Please tell everyone not to let Olivia hear of this. The last thing we need is for her to get upset and end up in A&E along with Adam.' His voice broke and he coughed as if to cover his shattered emotions. 'Jesus, Neva. I pray to God he's going to be OK.'

'He will be, Rafe. And with Hazel taking

care of him, we know he's in good hands. He'll be cracking jokes about this before we know it.'

'May I ask you to pack a few things for him, Mr Wynter?' Hazel said. 'Whatever it is, I'm pretty certain they'll keep him in for a day or two.'

'What? Oh yes. Of course. I'll do that now.'

Neva met Hazel's eye, and she saw that Hazel looked concerned, in spite of what she had said.

Either Hazel knew more than she was saying, or she was feeling guilty for not noticing that Adam was actually unwell, and it wasn't merely a chat up line, after all.

Chapter Twenty-One

'It's sepsis. But he's going to be OK.'

Rafe's voice sounded like an old man's when he called Neva at 2 a.m. but his sigh of relief was audible.

'They're sure? On both counts?'

'Yes. And Hazel knew it was. She just didn't want us to panic. I'm not sure whether to be cross with her, or glad she tried to make us think it could be something less dangerous. The doctor told me that her rapid response and initial treatment meant Adam will make a complete recovery. It was in the very early stage and he's incredibly lucky that there was someone who knew what they were doing. They've done scans and tests and there's no damage to any of his organs.'

Neva burst into tears. 'Oh Rafe! I'm so relieved. We've all been so worried. I wish I'd come with you. Are you OK?'

'I'm fine. Just tired. I wish you were here, too, although there's nothing either of us can do, so it's better that at least one of us can get some sleep. I'm going to stay until the morning. Hazel's also staying with him tonight. She's told the doctor she's the family's private nurse and that she'll be taking care of Adam when he comes home. They all seem to know her and have been happy to allow her to help attend to him. She said she hoped I wouldn't mind but this way, they'll keep her fully informed.' He gave a little laugh. 'As if I would mind. And Adam will be pleased. I think he's quite taken with her.'

'With Hazel? But he flirts with everyone. I didn't tell you this but he and Jo almost had a fling. If he hadn't been ill, they'd probably be in bed together right now.'

She didn't know whether she should have told Rafe that, but she wanted to lighten the mood now that they knew Adam was safe and out of danger, and with Hazel looking after him, they had nothing to worry about.

'Really? Well, he'll have everyone running around after him when he gets home. Olivia doesn't know, does she?'

'No. We've all made sure not a word reaches her ears. Although she did tell Judith that she thought she heard sirens. Judith told her it was probably a film the night duty nurse was watching on her iPad and Olivia seemed to accept that. I called Mum and Dad, and also Rowan and Nigel. I hope you don't mind but I had to.'

'Of course I don't mind. I know how anxious you must've been. I can't tell you how frightened I was. For one dreadful moment, I thought we might ... not be so lucky.'

'Do they know what caused it? How does someone get sepsis?'

'From an infection. Either from a cut or injury of some sort, or from an internal infection. They said Adam's immune system was probably weakened by the Norovirus, but the infection was from a small cut he had on his arm. I don't know how he got that. I don't remember him saying he'd cut his arm. But it could be from anything. There's lot of sharp corners in the old barn. And in the house, too. Hazel spotted it and treated it and they've checked it here. There was a tiny rash forming around it, Hazel has just told me, which is how she knew it was almost certainly sepsis. The doctor says Adam will be here for a couple of days and then it will possibly take anything from seven to ten days for him to make a full recovery. He's out of danger though. That's the main thing. I had no idea, but thousands of people die from sepsis every year because it's missed or misdiagnosed. As Hazel told us, the symptoms are very similar to the flu and if people don't seek help in time it can lead to multiple organ failure and death fairly fast. But like Adam, many more people are cured of it, provided they get help in time.'

'I didn't know that either. Thank God for Hazel then.'

'Amen to that. But I've told her that from now on, she must tell me the complete truth if she suspects a member of my family, or anyone at Wynter House, has a life-threatening condition.'

'Let's hope that won't happen. I think there's been enough drama around here to last a lifetime, don't you? It seems to be one thing after another.'

'Yes. It hasn't all been bad though. I met you and fell in love. That makes up for all the other things that have happened.'

Neva hesitated. 'Rafe? I know this isn't the time to discuss this, but has what happened today, and with Olivia, made you think any more about meeting your sister, Catherine, and your niece? I mean, thankfully, Adam's OK, but if he hadn't been … I'm just saying that sometimes we shouldn't put things off. We never know what's waiting around the corner.'

'I know. You must be able to read my mind. I've been sitting here thinking something similar. But it'll have to wait until both Olivia and Adam are fully recovered. I'm not taking any chances with their health. Now get some sleep. I don't suppose you've been to bed, have you?'

'Actually, I'm in Jo's bed with her, but now she's fast asleep. We've been chatting about our move to Merriment Bay to try to take our minds off Adam. Now I know he's OK, I'll leave her a note and go to your room.'

'I won't be back tonight.'

'I know you won't. You said that. But you don't mind if I sleep there anyway, do you? I'll feel happier if I'm there.'

His voice softened considerably. 'And I'll feel happier knowing that's where you are. I was hoping you'd be there every night, Neva. I hadn't thought about your flat in Merriment Bay. I know that sounds selfish, but it's true. I think I'd assumed you'd commute the five miles every day. But I suppose that's unreasonable of me. Perhaps we should discuss it over the next few days. There's no reason why I couldn't come and spend the night with you in your new flat and drive the five miles to and from Wynter House.'

'Or why we shouldn't spend a night apart every so often.'

'Oh? That I definitely hadn't considered. Would you want to do that? Sorry. That sounded pathetic, didn't it? I think I'm just so glad we're together that I hadn't considered we'd ever be apart.'

'Not apart, exactly. Just not in the same bed every night. But we're both really tired. Let's discuss it face to face, as you said. I love you, Rafe. And I'm so happy that Adam is going to be all right. Give him my love in the morning.'

'I shall. And I love you. Good night, Neva. I'll see you tomorrow.'

Neva made a sort of muffled shriek as the call ended. It was partly due to relief and partly due to the pent-up fear and realisation that Adam might actually have died, if it hadn't been for Hazel.

'OK.' Jo sat up once Neva had rung off from Rafe and she rubbed her eyes. 'I'm glad Adam's going to be fine. It sounds as if he owes that to Hazel. It also sounds, from what I heard of your end of the conversation, that it seems as if Rafe expects you to spend every night of your life with him. Clearly he has no concept of people sometimes needing their own space. But more importantly – and I'm leaving the best bit till last, you didn't tell me he and Adam have a sister and a niece. Is that what the big drama was that nearly killed Olivia?'

'Oh God, Jo! You weren't meant to hear that. I thought you were asleep. Whatever happens, please don't mention it to Adam or Rafe. Or anyone at all. I promised Rafe I'd keep the secret and he'll be furious if he finds out you know.'

'You can trust me, Neva. You know that. But now I need to know all the details. So come on. Spill. And don't leave out the goods bits.'

Chapter Twenty-Two

Ensuring Olivia didn't find out that Adam was in hospital meant lying about where Hazel was the following day.

Rafe's initial idea, when Neva joined him at the hospital early that morning to take him a change of clothes and his toothbrush, was to say that Hazel was unwell, but Neva said that wasn't wise.

'Olivia might refuse to have her back. You know Olivia doesn't really want her at Wynter House, so she'll use Hazel being ill as an excuse.'

'You're right,' Rafe agreed. 'She'll probably say I'm foisting a 'sick person' onto her and start telling me she feels unwell again herself. We'll have to say that Hazel had a family matter to deal with, or something along those lines. Although it might not be too much of an issue. We're going to see what the doctor on duty says today, and subject to that, Hazel will either return to Wynter House or stay here a little longer with Adam. She says the agency will send another nurse if we feel one is needed until she returns. I'm just going back in to see if Adam is awake. As it's out of hours, you may have to stay here in the waiting room. Is that OK?'

'Of course. I'll be here when you get back.'

He was back within a matter of minutes and Hazel was with him. Adam was still asleep and as they discussed the best course of action, Hazel made it abundantly clear that she didn't want to be a party to any lies. No matter how small or well-intentioned.

'I understand the problem,' she said, sitting in the waiting room with Neva and Rafe. 'But I'd prefer not to lie. Honesty is something I feel very strongly about. However. I am prepared to bend the truth a fraction in the circumstances. Perhaps we could say that another patient required my services and that as Mrs Wynter and I hadn't yet formed a bond, we thought it wouldn't make a difference to her who her care provider was, whereas my other patient had requested me, specifically.'

'I like your thinking,' Rafe said, grinning at her and also at Neva. 'Although, forgive me for questioning this, but isn't that also a lie? Adam hasn't specifically requested that you take care of him.'

Hazel grinned back. 'Actually he did. He asked me himself if I would give him a quick once-over.' She suddenly became serious. 'I wish to God I had done so right away. But I thought he was flirting with me. I didn't realise he was genuinely unwell. I'll never forgive myself for failing to notice that he was. I would completely understand if you decided to ask me to leave and to hire someone else.'

'You can't blame yourself for that, Hazel,' Rafe said, looking somewhat surprised that she'd said it.

'No, you can't,' Neva said. 'And if anyone is to blame for that it's me and Jo. We were the ones who made you think that Adam was a flirt. I'll explain it to you later, Rafe. Let's just say that Hazel was in no way at fault. And no one else noticed he was ill either, at first. It was only after Hazel had left the room and you arrived, Rafe, that there appeared to be anything wrong. And then it all happened so suddenly. Plus you did save his life, Hazel.'

Rafe gave Neva an odd look, but agreed. 'You weren't at fault, Hazel. Adam had been perfectly healthy during lunch. You had no reason to suspect he was unwell. And he does like to flirt, so it's perfectly understandable, especially as I can imagine the way he might have phrased his request. Please dismiss such thoughts from your mind. As Neva said, you saved his life. Things could be considerably worse if you hadn't acted so fast. I have no intention of replacing you as his nurse, or as Olivia's. Although whether you are prepared and willing to be both, is a separate issue.'

She immediately confirmed she was happy to do so, but Neva didn't think Hazel would dismiss the guilt she clearly felt, quite as quickly.

What was most surprising was that Olivia did seem to care who her nurse was.

'She said we should've checked with her before we agreed to let Hazel go running off to some other patient,' Rafe told Neva that night when they finally got some time to sit and relax. 'She was also furious that I hadn't been to see her before this evening and that I'd left it to Judith to break the news. I do feel guilty for that. Not with regard to Olivia, but for Judith. I can imagine what she has had to contend with all day. And the replacement nurse the agency sent, almost walked out after spending an hour with Olivia. It took both Judith and Archie to persuade her to stay. I should've returned from the hospital and told Olivia myself.'

'You can't be in two places at once, Rafe. If you're not careful, you'll end up in hospital too, the rate you're going. Dashing there and back and then trying to calm Olivia before racing over to the distillery to see how things are going there in your absence is one thing. Having to allay everyone's fears about whether or not sepsis is contagious, then bolting down some food and driving back to the hospital again to get the results of the further tests the doctors suggested, must have been exhausting.'

'But at least it was good news, so it was worth it. And to see Adam open his eyes and smile, definitely made it worthwhile. It won't be long before he can come home, so the doctors say. Which also means Olivia will get Hazel back. On a part-time basis, of course. We're still maintaining the story of Hazel having another patient. And it's true, which makes it even better.'

'Well now I think you need a good night's sleep.'

'What I need is one of your cuddles. And several of your kisses. Although I'll happily agree to an early night, if you will.'

Neva laughed. 'How on earth have you got the energy for that?'

'From you. I feel as if I get a shot of adrenalin every time I look at you.'

'People do say, love cures all ills. And I do love you, Rafe. More than you can imagine.'

'I can imagine a lot. And right now, I'm already imagining what I want to do tonight.

'Then let's go upstairs right now before anyone realises you're back and asks you to do something else.'

Hand in hand, they got up from the window seat in the library, where Neva had been reading and waiting for Rafe to come home, and walked into the hall.

'Rafe?' It was Amelia's voice. 'You're back.

I need to speak with you.'

Rafe hesitated for a moment. But only one moment.

'I'm sorry, Amelia, but it'll have to wait until tomorrow. Or you can discuss it with Sean. I'm afraid I'm required elsewhere on a rather urgent matter.'

Without waiting for a reply, he and Neva hurried up the stairs.

Chapter Twenty-Three

Neva knew packing up her things from her flat in London wasn't going to be fun, but doing so when she'd rather be back at Wynter House with Rafe, made it even less so.

But she had to do it. She couldn't leave it all to Jo. That simply wasn't fair. She already felt she'd let her parents down by not helping them with their move from Surrey to Merriment Bay on Wednesday.

'Don't give it another thought,' both Dawn and Dennis said, via speakerphone the day before their move. 'The removal men are doing everything, and Rowan, Nigel and Sasha will be coming over to help. Rafe needs you there at Wynter House to give him some emotional support at such a time. We're so relieved to hear that Adam's going to be OK. Will he be out of hospital soon?'

'In a day or two, we think. Are you sure you don't need me?'

'We're sure. You take care of Rafe. And yourself, of course. We'll see you once we're in the new house in Merriment Bay. It's all getting very exciting. We've lived in this house for most of our lives and we're looking forward to our new start. And to breathing in the sea air every day. Although Rowan's been a little tearful about us moving so far away. We keep telling her it's really not that far. Sasha, on the other hand can't wait for us to move. I think she sees it as an opportunity to return to Wynter House. She hasn't stopped talking about the place since the minute we all left.'

Rowan said the same when Neva called her later.

'You stay there,' she said. 'Everything's under control as far as Mum and Dad's move goes. I wish I could say the same about Sasha. She goes on and on about wanting to move to Merriment Bay so that she can spend more time at Wynter House. She wanted to live there, of course, but we've finally got through to her that is something that is never going to happen.'

'Would you and Nigel consider moving down to Merriment Bay? Dad did say at Christmas that you could run the firm from anywhere. And once Rafe's new business is up and running, and money is coming in, I know he'd be only too happy to employ Grey Building & Design to work on Wynter House. He was very impressed with the work Nigel and Dad did while you were here.'

'We've been discussing it, to tell you the truth. The closer Mum and Dad's moving date got, the more I realised how much I was going to miss them. And not just me. Sasha will miss them too. And Nigel. The thing is though, we'd have to put our house on the market and then find somewhere down there. We could appoint a manager to run things up here and, as Dad suggested, run the rest of the business from Merriment Bay. But we glanced in the estate agents when we were there and the only suitable houses were miles away from the village. It seems it's such a beautiful place to live that no one wants to leave.'

'Once we're all settled in, we'll keep our eyes and ears open and let you know if anything comes up. If you register with the agents who dealt with Mum and Dad's new house and get to know them, they may call you first if something does come to the market. It would be wonderful to have the entire family in Merriment Bay. Especially now Jo is going to be there too.'

'I think it's going to happen. I've got a good feeling about it. But first we need to get Mum and Dad moved in. And before you ask again. No. We don't need you to come and help. You concentrate on Rafe, and on getting yourself and Jo moved down from London. And if you need any help with that, Sasha's more than happy to take a day off school.'

'Thanks. But I think Jo and I can manage.'

Neva was excited by the prospect of having all her family, and her best friend, not to mention her new boyfriend, Rafe, all living in such close proximity. She would have a word with Rafe, and also with Adam, when he was better. They had said the estate agents in Merriment Bay were friends. Perhaps a word or two from Rafe and Adam might help secure first viewings of any properties for sale, for Rowan and Nigel.

That thought helped to assuage her guilt a fraction. Not that she really had cause to feel guilty and it did sound as if her family had everything under control.

Her parents' move went smoothly and without a single hiccup. The removal men did all the work and Rowan and Nigel, and Sasha too, had been on hand to help, at the Surrey-end of the move, as Rowan had said they would. Although quite how much help Sasha would have been was questionable. But at least the fact that they'd all spent the morning with Dawn and Dennis meant a lot to Neva.

She and Jo had driven to Merriment Bay to Dawn and Dennis' new home to lend a hand in the afternoon and to help with the unpacking. Jo couldn't believe her eyes when they drove down Channel View Lane, the narrow road that separated the modern, architect-designed house from the shingle and sand beach and the sea, directly opposite. Other than a small drive and front garden, the front door opened onto the wide expanse of beach.

She was equally astonished when they went inside.

'This place is the complete opposite of your parents' house in Surrey. This looks as if it's been beamed down by aliens from some far off and far-advanced planet.'

'I know.' Neva smiled. 'When Mum and Dad showed us the place at Christmas, we all said the same. Each of the four bedrooms is en suite and has a view of the sea. The master bedroom has views to the front and the side, overlooking the bay in the distance. There's a study, a small library, a family bathroom, and a lift. And wait until you see the massive, open roof terrace. It's got plants, sun loungers, chairs and tables, and astonishingly, a hot tub. Imagine sitting in that on a hot summer night and staring up at the stars.'

'I hope Dawn and Dennis are prepared for lots of visits from us,' Jo said, winking. 'I really like the sound of that.'

Rafe had joined them for a celebratory drink that evening, and he too had been impressed by the house. Especially the hot tub. But he had only stayed a while. He wanted to be at the hospital with Adam as much as possible. Adam's close brush with possible death seemed to have made Rafe feel rather protective of his brother.

'Not that he really needs me there,' Rafe said, to Neva, Dawn and Dennis as he was leaving. 'Adam doesn't appear to have any concerns about how things could have easily been so different if Hazel hadn't acted so promptly. Since waking up and finding himself in hospital, with Hazel taking personal care of him, he seems perfectly happy to be left alone with his nurse. In fact, I think my visits probably cramp his style. But I have to go and see him. I know this sounds ridiculous but until he's home at Wynter House, I won't be entirely convinced he's completely out of danger.'

Neva smiled. 'I understand that. But I'm beginning to think that, like Adam suggested Olivia was doing, he himself is making the most of the situation. You said you thought he was interested in Hazel. Perhaps he's using this time to break down her defences.'

Rafe grinned. 'I don't think it's working. Hazel is as professional as ever. She's told him more than once that she has no time for his nonsense. But he has said several times that he'd rather be at home in his own bed, with Hazel looking after him, than in the hospital. And as he grins every time he says it, I think we can be certain he's definitely recovering well. He should be home by tomorrow.'

And he was. The hospital discharged him first thing on Thursday morning and Hazel and

Rafe had him back at Wynter House and tucked up in his bed well before lunchtime, leaving Rafe free to spend the rest of the day in the distillery, with Amelia and Sean.

Neva and Jo left for London early on Friday morning and within a couple of hours, Neva couldn't wait to get back to Wynter House.

'I can't believe how much I miss the place already.'

Jo threw her an odd look. 'How are you going to feel when the flat completes and it's free for us to move in? Are you sure you'll want to go and live there? Or will you want to stay at Wynter House?'

'I haven't really given it much thought. Rafe had assumed I'd stay with him and commute to the salon but I had assumed I'd live in the flat and go and spend the night with him on a regular basis. We were going to discuss it properly but we still haven't got around to it. There's been so much going on. And speaking of things going on, are you ever going to tell me where you kept dashing off to during the last few days? Every time I looked for you, you were nowhere to be found.'

'That's not entirely true. We've had a lot of time together and we spent all of Wednesday afternoon with your parents. But Rafe needed you far more than I did, and you were helping Judith quite a bit. I think you're getting into the role of mistress of the chatelaine.'

'Hardly. But the time seemed to fly and I can't believe we're back in London, packing up our old lives for the final time and about to embark on a new adventure. Can you?'

'No. But at least I'm pretty certain that this time I move, it won't turn into a complete disaster.'

They glanced around the flat and at the pile of boxes. Rob had brought the rest of Jo's things over from his house and dumped them in the middle of the sitting room. They'd forgotten he still had a key. He had texted Jo to tell her what he'd done, late on Thursday night, which meant a call to the removers on Friday morning to tell them that the detour to Upminster wasn't necessary, after all.

'You still haven't told me where you went off to,' Neva persisted. 'Have you been spending time with a handsome estate manager we both know?'

Jo shook her head. 'No. Sadly not. Gavin seems to be avoiding me whenever possible. Since the day we met, that day he overheard our conversation about Adam, he's looked at me as if I'm the last person on the planet he'd want to spend his time with. You'll find this hard to believe, but I've actually been with George.'

'George? As in the former estate manager and gardener? Er. You do know he's in his seventies, don't you? He's not your usual type. I thought your plan was to have as much fun as possible at Wynter House.'

Jo grinned. 'I'm well aware of his age, and it's not like that. As for me having fun. Oddly enough, I have. George is a very interesting and knowledgeable man. His stories about the past are fascinating. He has a way with animals like no one I've seen before.'

'I know. He was brilliant with Tempest.'

'Over the last few days, he's taught me more about life in the country and about managing the land than I ever thought I'd want to know. If you'd told me I'd look forward to spending my days with a seventy-something man, with a slightly stooped back and hands as rough as leather and a laugh to match, I'd have said you were mad. And before you jump to conclusions, I only know his hands are like leather because he held my hand when we were climbing up a tree.'

'You climbed a tree? Seriously?'

'Yep. We climbed a tree. Not very high. Only a few feet off the ground. But it had the most amazing view right down to the sea, five miles in the distance. I'll show you when we get back. And he's taught me which birds nest where. How to tell which animal has been around just from its tracks, and what the seasons mean to country folk. I'd now make an excellent farmer's wife. Should there be any gorgeous farmers in the vicinity.'

'Or the perfect estate manager's wife. Is that what you're aiming for, Jo? Have you fallen for Gavin Boyd? He's almost ten years older than us.'

Jo tutted. 'I haven't fallen for Gavin. I told you, the man's avoiding me. He's handsome though, but as I've said, several times I believe, I don't want to be anyone's wife. The farmer comment was just a joke. But I have fallen in love with something. And I definitely never thought you'd hear me say this. I've fallen in love with the countryside. I thought I might miss the bright lights of London, the wine bars, the theatres, the shops. But I think I'm going to be very happy in Merriment Bay and George says there's loads more he can teach me. He did say that Gavin could teach me too. But I don't think there's much chance of that.'

'I could ask Rafe to put in a good word with Gavin if you like.'

'No! If the man doesn't like me, I certainly don't want him to feel he has to be nice to me because his boss has told him to. Let's not talk about Gavin. Let's talk about something nice while we wait for the removal men to arrive.'

They didn't have long to wait. The doorbell rang a second or two after Jo had finished that sentence.

Chapter Twenty-Four

Adam was released from hospital and returned with Hazel and Rafe, to Wynter House just a few hours later. Rafe phoned Neva to let her know and also to see how things were going.

'It's all going pretty smoothly here,' she said. 'These removers you arranged for us are brilliant. Everything's packed and ready and we're all just taking a tea break. After we've finished our tea and biscuits, we'll be on our way back to Wynter House. We'll be there by early afternoon at the latest, I should think.'

'I'm pleased to hear that. I've told the guys where to put everything, so when you get back, you can leave it all to them. Just let them know if there's anything you or Jo need to have with you in your rooms, and they'll organise that.'

'Thanks. We've decided to leave everything packed, other than clothes and a few personal bits and bobs. I spoke to Dad this morning and he thinks we may be exchanging contracts on the salon and flat on Monday and we may be able to complete by the end of next week.

There's really no point in me and Jo unpacking for just a few days.'

'That is good news. Although we still haven't discussed whether you'll be living in the flat or staying at Wynter House. But I get the feeling, you're intending to move into the flat, aren't you?'

Neva hesitated for a second and moved away from Jo and the removal men to get some privacy.

'I think I should. I can't let Jo move to Merriment Bay on her own. And Dad has bought the place for me, so it doesn't feel right if I don't move in, at least for the time being. But that doesn't mean we won't still be spending most nights together, Rafe. Because we will. Assuming that's also what you want to do of course.'

'Do you really need to ask? If I had my way, you'd never leave Wynter House again.' He laughed suddenly. 'Oh dear. That sounded rather creepy even to me. But we should discuss this face to face, I think.'

'We should. How's Adam settling back in? Does Olivia still have no idea he's been in hospital until today?'

'None whatsoever. Hazel did tell me today that every time she came back to Wynter House to look after Olivia for a few hours, Olivia gave her the third degree regarding 'this other patient', but Hazel informed her that patient confidentiality meant that she couldn't divulge any details.'

'That must've made Olivia cross. Poor Hazel.'

'I'm sure it did. But Hazel seems perfectly able to cope with any eventuality or mood. I'm beginning to believe she may be the female and medical equivalent of Archie. Nothing ruffles her feathers. And talking of that, Adam's flirting doesn't appear to be having the slightest effect on her. But he asked me the strangest question today, once Hazel was out of earshot.'

'Oh really? What was that? Or can't you tell me?'

'He didn't swear me to secrecy,' Rafe said, laughing again. 'But it did take me by complete surprise. He asked me when and how I knew I'd fallen in love with you.'

'He did?'

'Yes.'

'And what was your reply?'

'I told him that I thought it was from the first moment I saw you. But that I didn't want to admit that to myself until a few days later. And even then, I couldn't quite believe it. I said I knew it was love when I realised that just a smile or a glance from you, made my heart beat faster, my spirits soar, and my skin tingle in a way I'd never felt before. Not even with Pippa. I actually felt a pang of jealousy if you smiled at anyone else. And I wanted to see you and talk to you, or just be close to you, as often as I could.'

'Oh, Rafe. That's so wonderful. And it's made me wish I was close to you right now, Rafe Wynter, and not some seventy-odd miles away.' She let out a sigh and gave a little laugh. 'What did Adam say to that?'

'He said – and please excuse the swear word, "Holy shit. I think I may be in trouble." And that can only mean one thing.'

'That Adam thinks he may be in love?' Neva definitely couldn't believe that.

'Precisely.'

'Or it could mean that he's still not completely well. And that he's having delusions or that the medication he's been on is having weird side effects.'

Rafe laughed. 'I suppose that's a possibility. We'll have to wait and see. The problem is, if he has fallen in love with Hazel, he may be in for a nasty surprise. And a lot more pain than he's ever experienced before. So in a way, I think I'd rather it was his medication.'

Chapter Twenty-Five

On the Monday after Neva and Jo had their belongings moved into storage in a couple of the empty rooms at the back of Wynter House, contracts were exchanged on the flat and salon in Merriment Bay and completion fixed for a few days after that, as all parties were eager to get things finalised.

By Friday the 17th of January, Neva and Jo were on the move again. This time to Merriment Bay.

They could have completed on the following Monday and given themselves another weekend at Wynter House, but Neva had read that it was unlucky to move home on a Monday.

'After everything that's happened since that Friday before Christmas when I drove down to stay at the cottage in Wyntersleap with my family, I'm not taking any chances,' she said.

Jo fell in love with both the salon and the flat as soon as she saw them. Neva had shown her the outside and they had both peered in the window of the closed salon. The owner had decided not to reopen on her return from her Christmas holiday in Spain, once she was told that the purchasers, namely Dawn and Dennis Grey, were eager to exchange and complete as quickly as possible.

Jo had marvelled at the large gold-painted pillar which separated the entrance to the salon and the bright blue door to the flat upstairs.

'This looks like one of those things a pole-dancer might use. Only bigger. I like it!'

Two large picture windows either side of a central glass door with a tinkling bell above it, fronted a spacious reception area in which there was a desk, shelves for product displays, and a comfy-looking, multi-coloured sofa that had been left by the previous owner. There was also a gold leaf, metal and glass, coffee table, scattered with, now dust-covered, magazines.

The salon had deep red walls and it contained three retro black faux leather chairs in front of three black dressing-table type units. Each one had a grand, gold-leafed framed mirror sitting on top. Opposite, were a line of five fake, orange trees. These marked the border between the cutting and styling area from three wash basins with three, black faux leather, reclining chairs. At the end of the salon, were two doors, each leading to beauty rooms. One had a treatment table matching the salon chairs and the other had a luxurious-looking massage chair and add-on foot bath for pedicures. There were also a couple of table and chairs for manicures.

'I'm not sure about the walls,' Jo said. 'Other than that, it's fantastic. And with the furniture and fittings left in place, it's ready to go. This is really wonderful, Neva. I'm so excited.'

'I love the red walls, but I agree they don't work in this space. As we can see the sea from here, I think they need to be much lighter and brighter. So should the tables. I want to bring the outside in. I'd like this to be a place of relaxation.'

'You're keeping the gold leaf though, aren't you?'

'Oh yes. I think we all need a bit of gold in our lives.'

Jo screamed in delight when she saw the flat, especially as Neva took her to it via a semi-hidden door leading from the salon into the long hallway and the flight of stairs, at the top of which was the door to the flat.

The building was situated on a corner and it had windows to the front and side. The kitchen at the side was large, light and airy. There was a good-sized bathroom to the left of that. On the other side of the kitchen was an even larger sitting room with two French windows leading out onto small balconies. One was at the side and the other, at the front. They were just wide enough for a bistro-type table and two small chairs, or possibly a small reclining sun lounger. The views from the balconies were idyllic. The bay sat to one side and in front was the English Channel.'

'Oh my God, Neva. I can see us now, sitting there after work, drinking Rafe's Wyntersleap Gin, or maybe a glass of wine or two, and taking in those views over a good-old gossip.'

'Both bedrooms also have stunning views. You can sit in bed with your coffee and watch the clouds roll in from the sea.'

Jo gave her a horrified look.

'Clouds! Forget clouds, Neva. From now on it's going to be sunshine every day.'

Neva really hoped Jo was right. But she and Rafe had still not fully discussed their plans, and for some reason, Neva had a feeling that when they did, things weren't going to be quite so sunny.

He'd already made it clear from their conversation on the day she and Jo moved out of the London flat, that he wanted her to effectively, live at Wynter House. That was a wonderful prospect, and one Neva wanted too, but she felt she needed some time with Jo, and also to live in the flat Dawn and Dennis had bought her. She knew they wouldn't be offended if she didn't, but in a way, she wanted to, even if it did mean she wouldn't spend quite so much time with Rafe.

Or perhaps she was seeing problems that weren't there. Ethel had told her over Christmas that she mustn't see shadows where there were none. Maybe she was doing that.

Rafe had told her several things about how his new, Wyntersleap Gin venture was progressing, although hearing about how incredible Amelia was on that front, she could have done without knowing.

She had told Rafe the things she was considering regarding the salon. Some of them she and Jo had discussed the night Adam was rushed to hospital.

'Have you had any further thoughts regarding the name of the salon,' Rafe had asked the night before she and Jo were due to move in.

'We're going to keep the name – The Mane Event for now. Partly because the locals all know it and partly because neither of us can come up with a name we both like at the moment. Once we're up and running, perhaps something will come to one of us. We're painting the walls a soft blue, although we're hoping to have a trompe l'oeil painted on one, or maybe two of them. Dad says there's one in the Italian restaurant he wants us all to visit when we celebrate our moves to Merriment Bay, when Rowan and the others next come down. He and Mum had dinner there the other night and he says the food is heavenly, too.'

'I know the place he means,' Rafe said. 'It's called Bella Vista. I've been there once or twice. The artist who painted the floor and walls is long gone though, I believe.'

'Yes. Dad asked the owner. But Dad told me that one of his new neighbours is an artist. He said he only met her briefly when she was taking photos of the sunrise the other day and although they chatted and she said she lived in one of the houses on his road, he couldn't remember her name, or in which house she said she lived. Not that there are that many along that road, but he'd rather wait and see if he spots her again before he goes knocking on everyone's doors to ask.'

'I didn't know any artists were living in Channel View Lane. But then again, the only people I do know who live there are the Lesters. I don't know half the people in Merriment Bay, to be honest. I don't spend that much time there. Adam and I did spend almost an entire summer on the beach once, when we were young. That's where we met Amias Wells. His dad, Alwick gave us lessons in windsurfing and sailing, although Amias taught us most of what we learnt. That's how we became friends. We don't see him as much as I'd like, either. But he has been running his own business since he was seventeen and after boarding school then uni, I had Wynter House to run, and Adam spends a great deal of his time in London. I can give Amias a call and see if he knows who this artist is. He knows everyone and everything in Merriment Bay and I haven't spoken to him since we were at his home on Boxing Day. Perhaps I'll invite him for dinner one evening. Although perhaps we should wait until Adam is fully recovered.'

'There's no urgent rush. We want to take our time settling in and sorting out the salon but we're thinking of opening around Valentine's Day.'

'No rush? You do realise that's only a matter of a few weeks away, don't you?'

'Is it? Oh yes. You're right. January seems to be going on wings.'

'We should do something special on Valentine's Day.' Rafe pulled her into his arms. 'Just you and me, Neva. We should forget about our businesses, this house, your flat. Even Adam and Olivia and Jo, and just spend some time together.'

'I'd like that. To be honest, a day just relaxing would be good. We've both been rushing around lately. If it was warmer, we could have a picnic by the Falls or something, but as it's probably going to be freezing in February, that's not such a good idea.'

'Unless you're Gavin.' Rafe laughed. 'I'll see if I can come up with something. But right now, I think we should make the most of our last night together before you move to Merriment Bay.'

'Last night together? What do you mean by that? That sounded rather dramatic.'

'Sorry. But I've been thinking about this for most of the day. I know we'll still sleep together most nights, and we'll see each other every day, but the thought of you moving out of Wynter House is affecting me far more than I thought it would. It's foolish, I know. And I'm sure in a week or two, I'll grow accustomed to it. But I'm afraid I simply can't help it. Perhaps it's because of what happened to my marriage, but I'm terrified of losing you.'

She wrapped her arms around him and squeezed him as tight as she could.

'You'll never lose me, Rafe. Ever. And I know I'm the one who wants this new arrangement more than you, but it's only for a while. Just until we settle in and get everything running smoothly. And you're not the only one who is worried. I'm leaving you here with Miss bloody perfect body. If anyone should be terrified of losing someone, it's me, of losing you to her.'

He looked genuinely surprised by that.

'Are you jealous of Amelia? There's really no need to be, Neva. I'd be lying if I said she doesn't have a good body, because I think we can all admit she does. But so do you, and more to the point, your body is the only one I'm interested in. And in case you're in any doubt about that, let me show you right now, just how much I love you and your beautiful body.'

By the following morning, all Neva's fears were swept aside, and so she hoped, were Rafe's.

The move went off without a hitch and by 7 p.m. on Friday evening, Neva and Jo sat in their new flat above The Mane Event, popping champagne corks. Well, Rafe was popping the corks. Neva and Jo were handing round the glasses of champagne to everyone who had helped.

'Why can't I have a glass of champagne?' Sasha asked with her usual sulky expression. 'I'm almost nine now.'

'Because we've given you a day off from school so that you could come and help.' Rowan rolled her eyes and sighed.

'And Rafe's kindly agreed that you can spend tomorrow at Wynter House, so that's two treats you're getting,' Nigel added.

Sasha grinned at that. She was probably already thinking up some trick to play on Carruthers, although everyone had told her that she had to behave because Olivia was still fragile and Adam wasn't yet up and about.

'But they're not going to die, are they?' was all she'd said to that. And she seemed a little disappointed.

'No,' Neva assured her. 'They're definitely

not going to die. They're both going to make complete recoveries, we're all very happy to know.'

'It's been one thing after another at Wynter House, hasn't it?' Rowan said.

'I know. But hopefully it'll only be good news from now on. Rafe's had to delay the launch of their gin, due to Olivia and then Adam being unwell, but Amelia seems to have used her contacts in the City and orders are already coming in. As much as I dislike the woman, she does seem to know all the right people.'

'Why do you dislike her so?'

'Mainly because she seems to like Rafe rather too much. I know that sounds stupid but every time I see her, she seems to have her arm through his or her hand draped over his shoulder. The worst part is, he appears to be oblivious to it. I mentioned it to him the other day and he was surprised. He said he hadn't noticed.'

'That's because he's so in love with you he doesn't notice other women.'

'Or because it feels so natural that he doesn't think anything of it. And that's not good.'

Despite the previous night, her worries were creeping back in.

'That's ridiculous. Are you jealous? Because I'm sure you have no cause to be.'

'Not jealous. Just concerned.'

'Again. No cause to be, I'm sure. If it makes you that uncomfortable, why don't you have a word with her about it? Tell her you'd rather she didn't keep pawing your boyfriend.'

'I think that would make her do it all the more. The worst thing is, Olivia seems to like her. Amelia's been "popping in to see her" apparently. She told us during dinner last night that she thinks Olivia is wonderful. When I asked Hazel about it, she said they were often deep in conversation. You know what that means, don't you?'

'Each to their own?'

'No. Well, yes. They are both alike. What I meant was, she's ingratiating herself into the family. If Olivia likes her, she'll no doubt be telling Rafe how much more suitable Amelia would be to be his girlfriend.'

'He's not going to take any notice of that.'

'Perhaps not. But when I'm down here at the salon, or in this flat, Amelia will be ensconced in Wynter House, with her feet well and truly under the table. She was only supposed to be staying for a week or so but it seems she's cancelled all her other plans, including her skiing trip, and is staying on for the foreseeable future.'

'But if she is getting Rafe sales for his gin, that can only be a good thing, surely?'

'Yes. But it also makes her even more

perfect, doesn't it? I'm no help at all when it comes to his business. Sometimes, when he's telling me about new mixes of botanicals they're trying out, it goes completely over my head. Amelia doesn't just understand what he's talking about, she's actually been making some suggestions of her own.'

'OK. Perhaps you do need to be a bit wary of her. Although I still don't think Rafe will be easily swayed. Now if it were Adam, I'd say you should definitely be worried. I can't imagine him settling down with one woman to the exclusion of all others, can you?'

'No. Although he's still flirting with Hazel, more so since he returned to Wynter House, even though he's getting absolutely nowhere. She's keeping things strictly on a nurse and patient basis and is treating him more like a troublesome schoolboy than an attractive and seductive man. When I visited him in his room, the other day, he actually asked me if I had any tips on how to get Hazel to like him.' Neva laughed at the memory. 'But I shouldn't really laugh. Rafe told me that he thinks Adam may be falling for Hazel in a big way.'

'Really? Wow. What did you say to Adam when he asked you?'

'I wished him good luck with that.'

Rowan rolled her eyes. 'Men, eh? They always want what they can't have. Until they get it, that is.'

Chapter Twenty-Six

It was the first night Neva and Rafe had spent apart since Christmas Eve – other than the night Rafe had spent at the hospital with Adam.

But that night didn't count because Rafe hadn't spent that night in a bed. This one he had. And he had spent it alone in his own bed. At least, Neva hoped he had. She was at the flat in Merriment Bay and he was at Wynter House, so she didn't know for sure.

No. That was ridiculous. Of course she knew. There was no way he would've spent the night with someone else. Not even with Amelia, no matter how much she might have tried. And Neva had a feeling Amelia would've tried.

Neva had wanted to ask him to stay at the flat. But it was her and Jo's first night in their new home and it didn't seem right after all the years she and Jo had been best friends, to leave Jo there alone, or to have Rafe there and still, effectively, leave Jo on her own.

Instead, Rafe had returned to Wynter Hose, although he hadn't left until almost midnight. And Neva and Jo had sat up and talked and planned and laughed, just like they used to in their flat in London. Then they'd watched the sun rise over Merriment Bay from the French windows of their sitting room, sprawled on their new armchairs, drinking champagne and eating leftover pizza from the Bella Vista restaurant.

'This is heaven,' Jo said, as reds and pinks and purples flitted across the sky.

'It is,' Neva agreed. 'but you know what a red sky means, don't you?'

Jo grinned. 'Yes. George told me. It means people are too superstitious for their own good and that instead of seeing a glorious, multi-coloured sun rise and a beautiful red sky, they see doom and gloom and despondency. But he also said it can mean we may be in for a spell of bad weather.'

'You really do like George, don't you?'

'Yes. I told you I did. Which is why I want us to have a proper moving in party and I want to invite him and everyone else I've got to know at Wynter House. Even Gavin Boyd. Although he'll spend the entire party avoiding me, I'm sure.'

'I'd like that too. Not Gavin avoiding you. I mean the party. And I agree that everyone from Wynter House should come. It'll have to be when Adam's better though. Although the doctors said he'd have made a complete recovery by now, Hazel says it may still take a week or two before he's back to his old self. He may have only had a very mild case of sepsis but even that can really knock a person for six, especially if they were already run down, according to Hazel.'

'We could make it a moving in party and a re-opening party for the salon. What about doing something for Valentine's Day? That's on a Friday this year. Or do you and Rafe have other plans?'

Neva smiled. 'We haven't set anything in stone but Rafe did say he wants us to do something special and for it to be just the two of us, so I think Valentine's Day is out. But maybe the Saturday would be OK. I'll speak to him today and see what he thinks, if that's OK with you?'

'It's fine by me. So what's the plan for today? I'll need some sleep before too long but I'll be up and about again by lunchtime. Are we going to make a start on reorganising the salon?'

'I think we should. This place is as good as done after everyone helped unpack and put everything away yesterday. I might nip over to Mum and Dad's for coffee. later. Or they might come here. And I'd like to nip up to Wynter House at some point during the day and say hello to Rafe. I know it's silly but I miss him already.'

'It's not silly. I miss Rob sometimes, and I'm not in love with him. I think I miss the habit. I'm not saying you and Rafe are a habit. You're in love. But we do get used to things being a certain way, very quickly, and not many of us like change. You've spent every night, bar one, with him since Christmas Eve. It's only natural you'd miss him.'

Neva's mobile beeped and she glanced at the screen.

'It's a text from Rafe. He says he's missing me and if I'm up, he'd like to come down and say hello. God, I love this man.'

'Tell him to bring some of Penny's delicious bagels and croissants, will you? Oh, and some of her heavenly marmalade. And a flask of that divine coffee would definitely hit the spot.'

Neva laughed. 'I'm going to call him and tell him what you said, but as far as I'm concerned, all I want is Rafe.'

Jo yawned and rolled herself off the armchair.

'I'll be in the shower. It's far too early to listen to all your lovey-dovey stuff. You might want to take a shower too before he gets here. I smell of pizza and dust and something I'm not quite sure I can accurately identify. I imagine you do too.'

Chapter Twenty-Seven

Life moved into a new routine. Neva and Jo spent their days at the salon, shifting furniture, giving the entire place a deep clean from top to bottom and getting into every nook and cranny.

The plastic plants would be replaced with stone pillars, and nearer to the opening day, topped with vases filled with flowers, or an ornament conducive to relaxation, like a Buddha, or a Roman or Greek goddess, or something similar; they couldn't quite decide.

But one thing they did agree on was the trompe l'oeil and that it should be of the sea and a sandy beach, perhaps with palm trees, or possibly with the Roman goddess, Venus rising from the waves in her seashell, with her long locks flowing in a summer's breeze, as she was depicted in Botticelli's famous painting. The implication of course, being that she was coming to the salon to have her hair and nails done, along with a wax, an eyelash and eyebrow tint, and anything else that sprang to mind. They wanted the place to be playful, yet serene.

A haven of tranquillity with a hint of fun.

Dawn and Dennis popped in frequently. Dawn brought delicious, homemade cakes, and Dennis did odd jobs around the salon and the flat.

'I thought I had come to Merriment Bay to retire,' he joked, 'not be the odd-job man at my daughter's new business and home.'

'You offered,' Neva said, laughing. 'And you bought the place for me so you've got no one but yourself to blame.'

'I blame your mother,' Dennis said, winking at Dawn.

Dawn smiled lovingly. 'You couldn't wait to get here and see what needed doing. Retire, my foot. You just wanted to live and work beside the sea.'

Dennis nodded and laughed. 'It's true. I'll admit that. Retirement seemed appealing but I'm already hoping Rowan and Nigel will move down and open a branch of Grey Building & Design in Merriment Bay where I can work part-time. Two or three days a week would suit me fine. And I'd love to do more work at Wynter House. I'd even be happy to work there for free. I don't suppose you could put in a good word with the owner, could you?'

He gave Neva a playful nudge.

'I'll see what I can do.'

Rafe spent his days at the distillery and as much as Neva hated to admit it, Amelia was opening doors for Rafe and Sean and Adam's, Wyntersleap Gin that the three men would never have been able to knock on, let alone open and be welcomed in.

The one thing Neva wasn't happy about was the date Amelia wanted to set for the official launch of the gin, especially as Neva had told Jo that they should keep the date free.

'Valentine's Day?' Neva queried when Rafe told her at the end of that first week. 'You're seriously telling me that Amelia wants to set the launch date for Wyntersleap Gin as the 14th of February?'

'I'm afraid so. I had no idea she was considering it until she told me today that's it's as good as arranged. I was as unhappy about it as you are, but what could I say? She has done so much to help us and it hasn't cost us a thing. She's setting up media coverage and arranging for buyers to attend. She's even got a luxury chocolate and confectionery manufacturer on board to make some gin-filled truffles in the shape of our bottles. And she's certain she can bring it all together in a matter of three weeks. I can't quite believe it. The thing that's worrying me right now is whether we can live up to all this hype. I'd imagined this all to be rather low-key. I feel completely out of my depth. But I am truly sorry about Valentine's Day. I'll make it up to you, I promise.'

'There's no need for that, Rafe. I do think

Amelia should've checked with you first before she started moving things forward. It is your business, after all. But if that's the date she wants, there's nothing I can say or do to change that. What sort of launch is she planning? Is it still lunch, a tour of the village and the Falls, followed by afternoon tea, a visit to the distillery and then cocktails?'

'Yes. But she says it needs to be an exclusive event, which means none of our current guests at Wynter House will be invited. I tried to get that changed but she says it's a deal-breaker. She's determined to create and maintain a certain image.'

'You don't sound convinced.'

He looked rather anxious and his brows knit together.

'Amelia's brought us orders we could never have achieved without her help. She's worked wonders in such a short amount of time. But I am beginning to wonder, if perhaps, Amelia's vision for our gin is very different to mine.'

'What do Sean and Adam think?'

'Sean feels the same as me. Adam says he hadn't given it any thought. Olivia is the one who has surprised me the most.'

'Olivia? You asked Olivia?'

'Yes. The copper pot still is named after her, and Amelia wants to do a photoshoot on Valentine's Day with Olivia, Adam and I standing beside it. We're all assuming that both

Olivia and Adam will be up to that, health-wise by then. Olivia thinks it's a wonderful idea. I don't remember the last time she was this happy. To be honest, I'm not sure she has ever been this happy. Apart from when my grandfather was alive of course. And I wasn't around to see that. She looks years younger, Neva. You wouldn't recognise how much she's changed in the space of a couple of weeks. Well, since Amelia arrived, in fact. They get on extremely well. That was another surprise. It's so good to see Olivia smile again.'

'Amelia seems to be a miracle-worker.'

'You sound cross. Are you very angry about Valentine's Day? I'm not sure there's much I can do about it, Neva.'

'I know. I'm not cross about Valentine's Day. It's really just a day like any other. But with overpriced flowers and gifts. We don't need that day to show one another how much we're in love, do we? We can do that every day of the year. I'm not cross about anything. I'm happy for you and for Olivia. Er. Will Amelia be leaving after the launch on Valentine's Day?'

'Oh?' He looked genuinely surprised. 'I don't know. I hadn't thought about her leaving. She's already talking about ideas she has post-launch, so I believe she may be planning to stay on for a while. Although what her other clients might think of that remains to be seen. I hadn't thought that far ahead to be honest. I think I've got used to having her around and it hadn't occurred to me to ask.'

That was something Neva definitely didn't want to hear.

'It's my fault, Jo,' she said that evening as she and Jo curled up with a pizza from Bella Vista and a bottle of rather nice wine.

'How is this your fault? The woman's a cow. That was obvious from day one.'

'But if we'd stayed at Wynter House, Amelia wouldn't have been able to spend so much time alone with Rafe.'

'How do you know she does spend any time alone with him? OK, they work together during the day, but they did that when we were there. Other than two evenings this week, and of course, tonight, either you've gone to Wynter House or Rafe has come here. And even on the two evenings you've spent here with me, you still went to Wynter House to spend the night. Later tonight, Rafe will be coming here to stay. So the only real difference is that we don't have our meals together now.'

'Or drinks.'

'But Rafe and Amelia still wouldn't be alone at drinks. Are you saying you don't trust Rafe?'

'No. I'm saying I don't trust Amelia. But when Rafe said that he'd got used to having her around, it felt as if a knife had been plunged into my heart.'

'OK. That's a bit dramatic, even for you. That doesn't mean he's used to having her around in a good way. A dog can get used to having fleas but it doesn't mean he likes them being there. Did he smile when he said it? Did his tone change?'

'No. He looked surprised though. And that's not good. And this thing with Olivia is the nail in my coffin. He did seem really pleased that she was happy again at last. And that is only because of Amelia.'

'I do agree that bit is rather annoying. But the truth is, Neva, there's nothing you can do about that. I think you need to tell Rafe how you feel. He did say that Amelia's vision for his gin and his vision weren't aligned. That's something, isn't it? He's not entirely bowled over by her.'

'Yet.'

Chapter Twenty-Eight

Olivia was now well enough to declare she no longer needed a nurse, and Adam too, was back to full health, so Hazel's services were no longer required.

And yet, Adam was reluctant to let her leave, which was of an equally great surprise to him as it was to everyone else.

He tapped on the open door of Hazel's room the night before she was due to depart.

'May I please have a word with you?'

She seemed unsure but after a while, which felt like an eternity to him, she shrugged.

'Of course, Mr Wynter. I'll be right out.'

'Or I can come in.'

Her eyes narrowed.

'Don't you ever give up?'

'Give up? I'm not sure what you mean.'

She marched towards him but he stood his ground.

And he handed her the bunch of flowers he was holding behind his back.

Hazel stared at them.

'They're for you,' he said, doubt and nervousness making him break out into a cold sweat.

'How kind.' She took the flowers and held them, heads down, in one hand, as if she was totally unimpressed. 'Thank you. Is that all?'

'All? Er. Should I have brought chocolates?' he quipped, wondering if he should have.

She smiled sardonically. 'I meant, is this what you wanted to have a word with me about? To give me these flowers, which I assume you asked Gavin to pick for you.'

'Gavin? No. I picked those myself just now. They're from the greenhouse on the other side of the kitchen garden.'

'Yes. I've seen them when I've been out for my walks. You picked them yourself?' She looked doubtful.

'Yes. I'm not completely helpless. And thanks to you, I'm back to full health.'

'It had very little to do with me, Mr Wynter. It's the hospital and the antibiotics you should thank.'

'I'm told that you were the one who diagnosed it. You saved my life.'

'I merely did my job. And not that well as it happens. I should've spotted you were unwell but I just assumed you were flirting with me as you do with everyone, it seems.'

'Ouch. OK. That's fair enough. I have been

202

a bit of a flirt, I'll admit that. But as for you not doing your job, that's ludicrous. You did save my life so please don't dismiss that as if it's nothing.'

'It's my job. I always try to save lives, if I can.'

'And you've been nothing but professional in your dealings with me, so as far as I'm concerned, you're excellent at your job. But here's the thing, Hazel. I'm well now and you're no longer my nurse. Or Olivia's. And I was wondering if, perhaps, you might consider going out to dinner with me.'

She gave a little gasp and blinked before her cool expression returned.

'Thank you, Mr Wynter. But no.'

'No?'

'No. And there's really no need. Or any point. If you feel you owe me anything, you don't. I've been paid for my services, thank you. And if you're asking me for any other reason, then I'm sure this may come as a surprise, but I have no interest in being added to your list, thank you all the same. Now if you'll excuse me, I need to get on.'

'No, Hazel. I won't excuse you.' He placed his hand on the door she was about to shut in his face. 'At least not until you tell me why it is you seem to dislike me so much. If you're not attracted to me, that's fair enough. Just say so and I'll leave you in peace. But I'm not sure where this hostility comes from. And it is hostility, Hazel. I've seen how friendly you are with others. It's only me you look at as if I've got some contagious disease and you need to keep as far away from me as possible. And we both know I haven't. Sepsis is not contagious. Have I done something to offend you?'

'Yes. You've treated me with the same contempt with which you seem to treat all women.'

'What? I don't treat women with contempt. And certainly not you.'

'You do. And you have.'

'When?'

'The minute you flirted with me and assumed I'd fall at your feet and succumb to your abundant charms.'

He blinked several times as he took that in and then smiled.

'Abundant charms? Does that mean you don't find me entirely unattractive?'

'Is that all you picked up from my comment? Why am I surprised? Please close the door when you leave.'

She turned away and walked over to the bed where her suitcase was only half-packed. She placed the flowers beside it, brushing the petals with her fingers as she did so.

'I chose the ones I thought you'd like.'

She whipped around to face him and scowled.

'I asked you to close the door.'

He grinned. 'You asked me to close the door when I leave. I haven't left.'

'So I see. Let me rephrase that. Please leave, Mr Wynter and close the door behind you.'

'Please stop calling me Mr Wynter, Hazel. I've asked you about fifty times each day to call me Adam and yet you won't. But you did just say you think I have abundant charms, so why is that? Are you putting up barriers, Hazel? Is that what this hostility is about?'

'You really are the most arrogant man I've ever met. You're treating me with contempt yet again. You're assuming that I've fallen for your charms and that I'm trying to keep you at arms' length so that I don't get hurt when you sleep with me and dump me. Has it occurred to you that not every woman will find you completely disarming?'

'Yes. Many times. But I'm not interested in every woman, Hazel. I'm interested in you.'

She gave another little gasp. 'For now. Until you get bored and move on to the next woman who takes your fancy.'

'No. I flirt, I've admitted that. And yes, I've slept with several women, mostly for fun and a good time, but they've always known that and felt the same. Unlike my brother, I've never been in love. In fact, I had to ask him what it felt like because I thought I might just have come down with something again. But from what he said, that's not the case. And although it's pretty clear you don't feel the same, I wanted to tell you how I felt. Partly because this is a first for me and partly because ... well, because I wanted to know if there was any hope at all that you might be prepared to give me a chance.'

'A chance? What are you saying, Mr Wynter? Is this another line? Are you actually trying to pretend that you think you may have fallen in love with me? Do you expect that to work?'

He moved closer and reached out his hand to brush a wayward strand of hair from her cheek.

'It's not a line, Hazel. I don't expect anything. And I'm definitely not pretending. Believe me, I don't want to feel like this. In fact, I think I've actually tried not to feel like this throughout my entire life. My parents split up when I was very young and my grandfather died long before I was born. Rafe's first marriage was a disaster. All my friends, apart from Will Lester, are single. What I'm saying is I haven't exactly been surrounded by people in loving relationships. As far as I could tell, love hurts. A lot. It's not something I wanted, or looked for, or felt I needed. Until I met you. And suddenly it's as if you alone can make the sun shine, and the birds sing and everything seem right with the world. OK. That does sound like a line. I'm not very good at this. Being honest and sincere, I mean. As I said. It's a first for me. But I'm not a bad guy really. I've got a good job. I'm not exactly ugly. I've got a flat in London but it's true that really, I still live in my childhood home. And that's not going to change any time soon. Unless you want it to. I've got friends who seem to like me. A brother who definitely does. Even Olivia thinks I'm OK. Just. All I'm asking is to take you out to dinner. One date. That's all. And if you don't enjoy the evening and you tell me to get lost. I'll go. Although I'll need you to recommend a cure for a broken heart. And that's not a line, Hazel. That's the complete and honest truth.'

She looked into his eyes and didn't say a word.

He met her look and they stood there in silence for several seconds.

A smile slowly crept onto her lips and without speaking, she shoved the suitcase off the bed, pushed him down onto it and straddled his hips.

'Hazel?' He wasn't sure whether she was going to strangle him or do something else entirely.

Her smile broadened. 'Don't look so worried, Adam. I'm a nurse. You're in good hands. It seems you may be suffering from something and I think it may be contagious. My diagnosis is, you need the kiss of life.'

He beamed at her as she leant forward and kissed him firmly on the lips, but after several seconds, he eased her away from him and looked into her eyes.

'Wait a minute. Did you just say it's contagious?'

She laughed and began to slowly undo the buttons on her blouse.

'Extremely. I think I caught it not long after I arrived and I've been fighting the symptoms ever since. I think the only way to treat it is to share some bodily fluids.'

'Hazel.' Her name slipped off his tongue like a sigh and a feeling like nothing he'd ever experienced shot through him. 'Whatever you say. You're the nurse. And I really don't want to kill the moment, but Olivia is next door. Perhaps we could continue this treatment in my room?'

She glanced towards the adjoining door and moved off him.

'That's probably a good idea. This may get noisy.'

He sat bolt upright. 'I'm really glad Olivia had a heart attack. I know that's an awful thing to say but if she hadn't, we would never have met.'

She grabbed his hands and yanked him upright.

'This isn't just a game, is it Adam? You look

sincere. You sound sincere.'

'I am sincere. It's not a game. Not for me at least. Please don't start having doubts.' He cupped her face in his hands. 'I'm pretty sure I love you, Hazel Smart. I honestly, genuinely think I do. And believe me, I'm as surprised about this as you are. More so in fact. And I don't think there's a cure in the entire world for this.'

He kissed her again and smiled as they eased apart.

'I'd like to sweep you up into my arms and carry you to my room. But the fact is, although I have recovered from the sepsis, I haven't fully recovered my strength. I'm not sure I can lift you.'

'Are you suggesting I'm too heavy? That I'm overweight and need to diet?'

She sounded as if she was scolding him but he could see the amusement in her eyes.

'No. You're absolutely perfect just the way you are. I'm too weak, that's all. And I can see from that smile and the twinkle in your beautiful eyes, that you were teasing me. You were, weren't you? Or have I misread that entirely?'

'I was teasing you. But I hope you're not suggesting that I should carry you. You may be weak but you're still too heavy for me to lift.'

'I suppose we'll both have to walk then.'

'Or jog. I've been telling you that's

something you should seriously consider to get your fitness levels back.'

'You have. That's true. But I've got an entirely different form of exercise in mind, and unless I was hallucinating just now, I think that you have too.'

Chapter Twenty-Nine

'Amelia's lovely, Rafe,' Olivia said when he went to visit her the following day. 'And exceedingly good at her job. There's nothing quite as attractive as a beautiful and intelligent woman, in my opinion. She also knows all the right people. She's extremely well-connected. You've had several orders thanks to her, I believe.'

'You're certainly well-informed. Yes. Amelia's been a great help. But so has Neva.'

'Neva? What has she done to help?'

'She's supported me, been there for me, given me more love and affection than I had ever imagined possible and has faith and trust in me.'

'A lot of good that'll do you. What you need is someone who is as clever as you. Someone who understands our world. Someone who moves in the right circles. And Amelia is far more attractive and graceful than Neva will ever be.'

'To you, perhaps, Olivia. Not to me. Neva

is clever. And as for understanding our world, I don't want to live in a world that's separate from other people. Those days are long gone. We're all equal now.'

'Nonsense. There will never be equality in the world. Only a fool would want that. If everyone is equal, who will do the work?'

'Even the Queen has a job. But I'm not here to discuss equality. I'm here to tell you that Adam and I have made a decision about our sister and our niece. We're going to invite them here for afternoon tea. We haven't decided when and we haven't been in contact yet, but I wanted you to hear it from us before we took things further.'

'You're making a mistake, Rafe. Where's Adam? If this is a joint decision, why isn't he here too?'

Rafe smiled. 'He'll be joining us soon, but he was ... otherwise engaged this morning. And I think he may have some rather surprising news of his own to share with you, Olivia. I suggest you prepare yourself for a shock. We don't want to have to call out another ambulance.'

'Shock? What kind of shock? What is all this nonsense, Rafe? You really have lost your reason since that chit of a girl arrived.'

'On the contrary, Olivia. I haven't lost a thing. But I have gained a great deal. Ah. Here's Adam now. This should be interesting.'

'Good morning, again, Rafe. Apologies for earlier.'

Rafe grinned at him. 'I should apologise, Adam. I did knock and I thought I heard you shout, 'Come in', but it seems I was mistaken.'

Adam burst out laughing.

'What *is* going on?' Olivia scowled at them. 'Adam? Rafe said you have something to tell me and I may need to prepare for a shock. Are you returning to London? That's hardly a shock. But as for meeting your half-sister, I've told Rafe it's a mistake and I shall say the same to you.'

'Thank you, Olivia. But we've made a decision and that's that. And I shan't be returning to London at the moment. In fact, I'm considering taking a sabbatical and helping at the distillery full-time for a while. Oh, and Hazel won't be leaving today, after all.'

'Hazel? Oh, that nurse. Why not? Is someone else ill?'

'Not ill, no. In love.'

'In love? What on earth are you talking about? Who's in love? And don't tell me that you are, Rafe, because you know how I feel about that girl. What does this have to do with that nurse?'

'I'm in love, Olivia.' Adam beamed at her. 'As it happens, with that nurse. And I'd like you to call her Hazel from now on. She's no longer an employee. She's now my girlfriend. And as surprising as it seems – especially to me, it's extremely likely that in the future, she may become much more than that. Although this is a first for me, and Hazel understands that. We're going to take it one day at a time and see exactly where it leads.'

The colour drained from Olivia's face. 'The nurse? You've fallen in love with the nurse? When? How could this possibly happen? Are you both trying to kill me? Has this entire house gone mad?'

'No,' said Rafe. 'This house hasn't gone mad at all. If anything, I'd say it's finally come to its senses. And we all hope you'll be around for many years to come, Olivia. Who knows, if we're very lucky, you may even live to hold one or two more great-grandchildren, but you'll definitely live to welcome your granddaughter, Catherine Devon and your first great-grandchild, Kyra to Wynter House. That much I can assure you.'

Chapter Thirty

'Hazel and Adam?' Neva said, shaking her head and staring at Rafe as he stood in the centre of a section of the salon, and told her and Jo the latest news from Wynter House. 'I still can't quite believe it, even though he did ask me several times if she'd said anything about him, or whether I knew what she thought of him. And I know you said you thought he'd fallen for her, but I had no idea she felt that way about him. I'm so pleased though. For both of them.'

'Not as pleased as I am,' Rafe said, pulling Neva into his arms and giving her a kiss. 'I wanted to tell you face to face.'

'I bet Olivia was thrilled,' Jo said, tugging another strip of wallpaper off the salon wall.

'Immensely,' Rafe said, laughing. 'Almost as thrilled as she was when we told her we were going to invite her granddaughter and her great-granddaughter round for tea. Oh. I'm sorry, Jo. You don't know we have a sister. ... Or do you?'

'I'm sorry, Rafe,' Neva said. 'Jo overheard

me on the phone that day Adam was taken to hospital. But…'

She glanced towards the salon door where Gavin Boyd was standing, a large pillar at his feet and his hands resting on the top of it.

'Gavin knows,' Rafe said. 'I told him on the way here. And there's no need to apologise about Jo. We're all friends.' He smiled at Jo and at Gavin. 'It'll soon be public knowledge in any event, if things go to plan. Of course we do need to take into account how our sister may feel about all this, before we go announcing it to the world. And then we'll have to make plans, just in case there's any fall-out from the scandal. Although I'm less inclined to think there will be. It is 2020, after all. Do you need some help?'

'Is that pillar for us?' Jo asked. 'Or are you just pleased to see me? Sorry. I don't know why I said that, Gavin. It was only a silly joke.'

'That's OK. And yes, this is for you. There're more if you want them but we only brought the one for now in case it isn't what you both wanted.'

'I love it,' Jo said.

'Me too,' said Neva. 'Are you sure there're going spare, Rafe? It's so beautiful.'

Rafe nodded. 'There are rather a lot of them all over the estate. Gavin or I can show you them.

Jo smiled. 'It's a replica of an Ionic pillar,

isn't it? And it looks like marble.'

'Yes on both counts,' Gavin replied. 'Where do you want it?'

'In that corner for now, please. Where we've already stripped the wall paper. But we may have to ask you or Rafe or someone strong to come back and move it. It looks heavy.'

He lifted it without too much effort and carried it to where Jo had pointed before standing to one side of where she stood.

'I'll give you my mobile number. Just call me if you need anything moved, or lifted, or anything else at all. I'm sure Rafe won't mind.'

'Not at all,' Rafe said. 'Call any of us, if either of you need anything.'

'I need some coffee,' Neva said. 'Dad's going to be here any minute. Mum's made some cakes. Will you and Gavin be staying?'

They both nodded.

'For a few hours,' Rafe said. 'And Adam and Hazel are going to pop in too. They're coming into Merriment Bay today to do a bit of shopping so I told them you wouldn't mind.'

'We don't mind at all. But what about Amelia? Won't she mind you being here and not all cosied up with her in the old barn?'

Rafe grinned and kissed Neva on the lips again and then he gave a small cough.

'I also have some news about Amelia. And I think this may come as a complete surprise. It certainly did to Olivia and it definitely did to

Amelia. To be honest, it even did to me, but I discussed it with Sean and with Adam and it seems we're all agreed.'

'What is it, Rafe?' Neva held her breath.

'Amelia has been brilliant and we can't thank her enough for everything she has done and the contacts she has given us, but her vision for our gin is not the same as ours. We want to make money, of course. But we don't see Wyntersleap Gin as the mass market product that Amelia wants. She said we'll have to build larger premises within a year. That's not at all what we had in mind. We see our gin as an exclusive brand. I told her this morning that I didn't think we were heading in the same direction and that it was best if we called it a day before she made any announcements regarding the launch. I'd already spoken to Will Lester and to the bank. We're paying Amelia a consultancy fee and basically, letting her go.'

Neva stared at him in astonishment and it was Jo who was the first to comment.

'Bloody hell. I bet she didn't like that.'

Rafe shook his head. 'She wasn't best pleased, I'll admit. She called me one or two choice names, in fact. But eventually she calmed down and saw things from our perspective. And it transpires that she hadn't fixed the launch date after all, and had only put out feelers for that date, so no harm has been done, either to our business or her reputation.'

'But I don't understand. You said that you'd got used to having her around and that she might be staying on. What has made you change your mind so suddenly?'

'You. I know Valentine's Day is just a day. But I want to spend it with you. And it's not just that. Olivia has been saying things that have made me think it might be more trouble than it's worth to keep Amelia around.'

'Oh Rafe! You didn't have to do that for me.'

'I didn't. Not entirely. I did it for me, Neva. And Olivia will get used to it. I also told her today that Adam might have died, and I honestly believe that we may be seeing a change in Olivia's behaviour from here on in. Of course I may be wrong. We'll have to see. But Amelia had to go as far as I was concerned. And the sooner the better, I feel. By tomorrow, we'll be saying goodbye to her.'

'But how can you afford to pay her? Sorry. That's none of my business.'

'It is. Or it will be in the future. I told you, I spoke to the bank and based on the orders we already have, they were happy to extend our loans to cover Amelia's costs. Which actually, weren't as high as they could've been. She did offer to continue and to do things our way, but to be honest, I'm growing rather tired of her constant pawing.'

'What?' Neva said, more surprised each

minute. 'I thought you were oblivious to that.'

'I tried to pretend it wasn't happening. After all, she was giving us her expertise for free at the time. I didn't want to offend her. But enough is enough. I'm not at all interested in Amelia.'

'That's called sexual harassment, Rafe,' Jo said. 'Women have been dealing with it for centuries.'

'Men have too,' Gavin said. 'Probably not as often, but it does happen.'

Rafe nodded. 'There's a diary at Wynter House of one of our ancestors who took a particular fancy to the gardeners on our estate. We had several back in the 1750s when the family coffers weren't so bare. It makes for very interesting reading. I learnt a lot about sex from that, at a very young age. She should've been one of those novelists who write erotica. She would've made a fortune. The men didn't dare say no, or they'd have lost their jobs.'

'So that's where you learnt your skills?' Neva said.

'Not all of them. But yes.'

'Was she married?' Jo said.

'Yes. But she had a very highly developed, sexual appetite.'

'A bit like me.' Jo grinned. 'Although oddly enough, I haven't been so interested lately. I've discovered there are other things that make me happy. I've been spending a lot of time with

George.'

'I did wonder about that,' Gavin said, throwing her a curious look. 'Shame you missed your chance with Adam.'

'She didn't,' Neva said. 'They both decided not to take things further.'

'What's this?' Rafe asked.

'I told you. I thought Jo and Adam might have a fling, but they decided they didn't want to, after all. Although it was the night Adam was ill, so that may have had something to do with it.'

'Oh I see. Well, don't worry, Jo. I'm sure you'll find someone who interests you before too long.'

'Perhaps I already have,' Jo said, darting a quick look in Gavin's direction. 'So, anyway. Amelia's really history then? I think we're all very glad about that.'

Rafe grinned. 'Amelia who?'

Neva threw her arms around his neck, stood on her tiptoes and kissed him.

The doorbell tinkled over the door and Dawn and Dennis stepped inside, carrying armfuls of bags and boxes.

'Hello you two,' Neva said, easing herself away from Rafe and beaming at her parents. 'Are they all cakes? Are we expecting an army?'

'Hello, sweetheart.' Dawn smiled as Rafe and Gavin took the bags and boxes from her and Dennis. 'And Hello, Jo and Rafe and

Gavin.' She kissed Neva on the cheek as soon as her arms were empty.

'Not an army,' Dennis said. 'But we did bump into that artist I mentioned. And when we told her about your salon and what you wanted, she said she'd be happy to have a chat with you although it's not her usual thing. But when I mentioned you'd got the idea of having either a Greek or Roman goddess from the statuary you'd seen at Wynter House, she was very interested and so was her daughter. When we said you were dating the owner, she was almost biting off our hands to meet you. I hope we haven't overstepped the mark. They should be here fairly soon. We told them to pop in around 11 a.m., which I hope is all right with you. Her daughter's an artist too.'

'Absolutely, Dad. Did you get her name this time?'

'Oh yes. It's Cat. Cat Devon. And her daughter's name is Kyra.'

'You have got to be joking,' Neva said, looking from Dennis to Rafe, to Jo and back to Rafe again.

'Joking? No. Why on earth would I be joking?'

Rafe looked stunned but he coughed and ran a hand through his hair.

'There's something I should tell you, Dawn and Dennis. It's a long story but I'll cut it short. Catherine Devon is, it seems, my sister, and

Kyra Devon is my niece. My father had an affair with Catherine's mother but we only discovered this on Boxing Day. I'd better call Adam and tell him to get here as fast as he can. If we're going to be meeting Catherine and Kyra, I'd rather we do so together.'

'Do you want to meet them like this?' Neva asked, as Rafe pulled out his phone. 'We can go upstairs and leave you and Adam here to meet them if you'd rather. Or you can go upstairs and we'll send them up to you.'

Rafe shook his head. 'No one needs to go anywhere. This has remained a secret for far too long. It's about time it all came out in the open. Adam and I were going to invite them to Wynter House, but in a way, this is far more casual. A chance meeting on neutral ground.'

'But it may be a shock to them if they don't know about you,' Jo pointed out.

'From what Dennis just said about Catherine – or Cat, as she called herself, seeming to be very interested when she heard Neva was dating me, I think we can assume that she might have an inkling that Adam and I exist and may be connected to her in some way. We'll soon find out. Ah, Adam. At last. I've got a surprise for you. We're going to be meeting Catherine and Kyra in about fifteen minutes at Neva's salon. I'll explain it all when you get here. Do you think you can make it here in time? Preferably, alive. Don't break any speed limits, or your neck. ... And yes. Of course you can bring Hazel.'

Chapter Thirty-One

Adam and Hazel only just made it. They arrived five minutes before the Devons. And it wasn't just Catherine and Kyra Devon who turned up. An older woman, presumably Mary Devon was with them, and to Rafe and Adam's obvious surprise, Amias Wells was too.

'Hello, everyone,' Amias said, as they all walked into the salon. 'I hope you don't mind me being here, Rafe and Adam, but Cat wanted me to come. This is Cat Devon, her daughter, Kyra and Cat's mother, Mary. And there's something you both need to know.'

'Those are the two men from Boxing Day,' Kyra said, pointing at Rafe and Adam.

'Yes,' Rafe said. 'And there's something you need to know as well.'

'Er. Unless I'm very much mistaken,' Neva said. 'I think they already do.'

'You know?' Catherine stared from Rafe to Adam.

'We found out on Boxing Day,' Adam said.

'Assuming you're all talking about the

same thing,' Mary Devon said.

'That we're your brothers, Catherine.' Rafe held out his hand. 'And your uncles, Kyra. We're both very pleased to meet you. Do you prefer to be called, Cat?'

'Oh my God!' Cat said, and suddenly burst into tears.

'Don't mind, Mum. She gets a bit emotional. We're both pleased to meet you,' Kyra said, taking Rafe's hand and shaking it and then shaking Adam's. 'I'm sorry if I was rude on Boxing Day but I had no idea who you were at the time. You see, we didn't know about you either until that same day. It seems both our families kept the secret.'

Cat turned to them and smiled, wiping away her tears with the handkerchief Amias gave her. She took their hands but to Neva's surprise, and obviously to Cat's, Rafe pulled her into a hug.

'I'm sorry,' he said, releasing her as quickly. 'I didn't mean to do that. But the excitement of meeting our sister has got the better of me.'

'Please don't apologise,' Cat said. 'I want to do the same.' She hugged him again and then she and Adam hugged. Then they hugged Kyra and before long, nearly everyone in the salon was in tears and everyone was introducing themselves and hugging and laughing and talking over one another.

'So you know our sister?' Adam said to Amias in shock and disbelief. 'It's certainly a small world.'

'Smaller than you think, Adam. Cat and I are in love. In fact. I've loved her all my life.'

He slid an arm around Cat's waist and the other arm around Kyra's shoulders.

'What?' Rafe said, laughing incredulously. 'How? When? Why didn't we know about any of this?'

'I think we all have a lot to discuss,' Amias said. 'And one or two confessions to make, which I hope we can all forgive and forget. Life's far too short to do otherwise, as we've recently come to realise.'

'I agree with you on that,' Rafe said. 'We were going to try to contact you, Cat and invite you to Wynter House for tea.'

Cat burst out laughing and looked at Mary Devon.

'Did you hear that, Mum? We've been invited to Wynter House for tea. It seems things are definitely changing.' She smiled at Rafe and Adam. 'Don't worry. That's a little joke between my mum and me. I have so many questions but I think I'm still in a state of shock. This isn't how I imagined meeting you for the first time.'

'Same here,' Adam said.

Rafe grinned. 'When Dennis told us who you were this morning, and that you were coming here, we did consider leaving. But only for a second. It has been too long. There didn't seem much point in waiting any longer.'

'I'm glad it happened this way,' Cat said. 'I asked Amias to come because I was nervous, but the moment we walked in, I felt completely at ease.'

'You burst into tears, Mum,' Kyra said, laughing.

Cat shrugged. 'I seem to do that a lot lately. But they're tears of joy, not sadness.'

'We heard about your grandmother,' Rafe said, now serious. 'I'm sorry for your loss.'

'Thank you. That was a dreadful shock. We had been estranged for years and I didn't get a chance to say goodbye. But that's another story and one that can wait. I have so much to tell you and so many questions to ask. And I want to hear all about you. I don't know where to start.'

'Let's start by sorting out some chairs and sitting down with a nice cup of tea,' Dawn said. 'And perhaps a slice of cake.'

'That sounds good to me,' said Cat.

'And to me,' Rafe said. 'After all. We've got to start somewhere. We've got our entire lives so far to catch up with, and our futures in which to do it.'

A Note from Emily

Thank you for reading this book. A little piece of my heart goes into all of my books and when I send them on their way, I really hope they bring a smile to someone's face. If this book made you smile, or gave you a few pleasant hours of relaxation, I'd love it if you would tell your friends.

I'd be really happy if you have a minute or two to post a review. Just a line will do, and a kind review makes such a difference to my day – to any author's day. Huge thanks to those of you who do so, and for your lovely comments and support on social media. Thank you.

A writer's life can be lonely at times. Sharing a virtual cup of coffee or a glass of wine, or exchanging a few friendly words on Facebook, Twitter or Instagram is so much fun.

You might like to join my Readers' Club by signing up for my newsletter. It's absolutely free, your email address is safe and won't be shared and I won't bombard you, I promise. You can enter competitions and enjoy some giveaways. In addition to that, there's my author page on Facebook and there's also a new Facebook group. You can chat with me and with other fans and get access to my book news, snippets from my daily life, early extracts from my books and lots more besides. Details are on the 'For You' page of my website. You'll find all my contact links in the Contact section following this.

I'm working on my next book right now. Let's see where my characters take us this time. Hope to chat with you soon.

To see details of my other books, please go to the books page on my website, or scan the QR code below to see all my books on Amazon.

Contact

If you want to be the first to hear Emily's news, find out about book releases, enter competitions and gain automatic entry into her Readers' Club, go to: https://www.emilyharvale.com and subscribe to her newsletter via the 'Sign me up' box. If you love Emily's books and want to chat with her and other fans, ask to join the exclusive Emily Harvale's Readers' Club Facebook group.

Or come and say 'Hello' on Facebook, Twitter and Instagram.

Contact Emily via social media:
www.twitter.com/emilyharvale
www.facebook.com/emilyharvalewriter
www.facebook.com/emilyharvale
www.instagram.com/emilyharvale

Or by email via the website:
www.emilyharvale.com

Acknowledgements

My grateful thanks go to the following:

Christina Harkness for her patience and care in editing this book.
My webmaster, David Cleworth who does so much more than website stuff.
My cover design team, JR.
Luke Brabants. Luke is a talented artist and can be found at: www.lukebrabants.com
My wonderful friends for their friendship and love. You know I love you all.
All the fabulous members of my Readers' Club. You help and support me in so many ways and I am truly grateful for your ongoing friendship. I wouldn't be where I am today without you.
My Twitter and Facebook friends, and fans of my Facebook author page. It's great to chat with you. You help to keep me (relatively) sane!
Thank you for buying this book.